surviving
the chase

By Lisa Renee Johnson

Dangerous Consequences

Surviving the Chase

surviving the chase

LISA RENEE JOHNSON

KENSINGTON PUBLISHING CORP.
www.kensingtonbook.com

DAFINA BOOKS are published by

Kensington Publishing Corp.
119 West 40th Street
New York, NY 10018

All Kensington titles, imprints, and distributed lines are available at special quantity discounts for bulk purchases for sales promotion, premiums, fundraising, and educational or institutional use.

Special book excerpts or customized printings can also be created to fit specific needs. For details, write or phone the office of the Kensington Sales Manager: Kensington Publishing Corp., 119 West 40th Street, New York, NY 10018. Attn. Sales Department. Phone: 1-800-221-2647.

Dafina and the Dafina logo Reg. U.S. Pat. & TM Off.

ISBN-13: 978-1-4967-0797-0
ISBN-10: 1-4967-0797-4
First Kensington Trade Paperback Printing: August 2020

ISBN-13: 978-1-4967-0799-4 (ebook)
ISBN-10: 1-4967-0799-0 (ebook)
First Kensington Electronic Edition: August 2020

10 9 8 7 6 5 4 3 2 1

Printed in the United States of America

For my mother.
Thank you for showing me what love is and for being my light-
house in the darkness. I am your reflection, the epitome of
strength, grace, and courage under fire. You stood so I could
stand. I am forever grateful.
To my father.
You came back for me. Thank you for teaching me that I am
worthy and I matter.
To my dad.
I feel your presence every day and I miss you.
Everything I am is because of all of you.

ACKNOWLEDGMENTS

I want to thank God for his continued blessings and for accepting me as I am and loving me anyway. It takes a village to raise a book and I want to acknowledge my village because without you *Surviving the Chase* would still be a figment of my imagination. As I type this, I'm ruminating on how political this exercise is for us authors. I mean, I want to thank each and every one of you personally by name, but that's not humanly possible since there are so many of you who play a significant role in my life and my author journey—plus they told me to keep this short. So it's almost midnight and I'm sitting here trying to decide whose name to list and I'm terrified I'm going to unintentionally miss someone and the truth is once it's in print there's no turning back. So here it goes.

To my husband, my three incredible sons and amazing granddaughter. Love is a verb and I'm overjoyed you were chosen to do this thing called life with me. I love you. To my awesome family, friends and fellow authors. Your generosity of love, practical advice and talking me off the ledge every now and again over a great cocktail is appreciated. You inspire me to be better. To my editor who has the patience of Job and my amazing Sunshine Squad who shouts my name from rooftops and encourages me to continue writing, I could not do this without you. And last but not least, the fabulous book clubs, booksellers, passionate readers, and YOU. Please accept these words as my personal gratitude to you for doing this "write" thing with me. Simply, I am because you are.

Now that that's out of the way, do me a quick favor and drop your name here: _____, you are my sunshine!

XOXO
Lisa Renee

Never chase love, affection, or attention. If it isn't given freely by another person, it isn't worth having.

—Unknown

CHAPTER 1

Payton Marie Jones propped her elbows on the adjustable waxing bed for a better view. Long brown legs resting wide open, she held her breath, anticipating the sting before she felt it.

"Relax, love," cooed the sexy service technician motioning for her to open her legs wider to give him better access. Payton did what he asked, then chuckled, wondering if this was what David Bryant meant when he invited her on this last-minute business trip, and insisted she take advantage of the decadent spa amenities.

The lavish décor, massage oils infused with diamonds, and the extensive menu of therapies and body treatments were just what she needed to exorcise a few demons out of her system. And the all-male service staff was a nice touch, definitely something you would only see in Las Vegas.

Eyes closed, Payton dipped her head back between her shoulder blades and inhaled the fresh scent of lavender.

"Ouch," she hissed on the next pull.

She still couldn't believe she had opted for this service, from a man no less, but since her usual esthetician, Kay, couldn't squeeze her in before her trip, what was a girl to do? Waxing her bikini area hurt like hell, but she couldn't imagine going without it. Besides her preference for being hairless down south, the waxing exposed numerous nerve endings that led to multiple orgasms, and the smoothness made her feel damn sexy. Hell, after a Brazilian, the mere act of crossing her legs turned her on. She opened her eyes and stared at the service technician as he winked at her.

For a white boy, he was damn fine. Deep-blue eyes, tall, muscular, and a rich golden tan that made him look as if he should be surfing on Venus Beach instead of locked away from the sun in the spa. He dipped the wooden stick into the pot of molten wax and spread it onto her skin in a figure-eight motion. Previously, after each pull, he briefly placed his hand over the freshly waxed area to stop the sting, but this time he followed the gesture with a kiss.

"You are so beautiful," he said in a thick European accent.

Payton detected a hint of nervousness in his voice, something she hadn't noticed until now. What the hell was he doing? Did he provide happy endings to all his clients? This was risky behavior and if she were him, she'd be nervous too. A single word to management about his little v-gesture and his ass would be fired on the spot. Then she remembered where she was and thought about the type of clientele that frequented this coveted spa and paid these outrageous prices. Those horny bitches wouldn't say a single word.

And today you're one of them, a tiny voice whispered in her head.

She glanced down at her smooth, caramel skin, then back at the shirtless man sitting between her anxious thighs. His sidelong glance was cautious as he traced his index finger along the freshly waxed landing strip and teased the tip of his finger in her warm, moist crease. He waited a moment, his eyes searching for the okay to coax open her folds, to touch the slickness pooling inside.

"You want to taste that, don't you?" she accused, clamping her legs shut around his hand.

"I want to make you come right now," he whispered. "Open your legs. Just a little bit."

She gazed into the shadows of his eyes, and he stared back,

shameless. He leaned in and with his free hand reached for the half-full champagne flute resting on the side table and handed it to her.

"Drink," he urged.

"Is this a part of the standard service?" she quizzed with a wide grin. "Or is my kitty irresistible?"

Payton took a swig of the champagne, warning bells going off in her head. She could hear her best friend, Sydney, chastising her about being overly friendly with her cookies, but she ignored it and tightened her thighs around his hand as her hips found their own rhythm. The one thing that she could always count on was crazy shit like this happening to her. Truth be told, she wanted to come, too. The craving was powerful, a magnetic pull forcing her hips to wiggle toward his hand like a heat-seeking missile. What was a girl to do? David was in all-day meetings, and if she didn't get a release right now, she'd have to make a detour back to the hotel room and get herself off or walk around for the rest of the day unable to concentrate, her thoughts dominated by that turned-on ache. In her mind, there was absolutely nothing wrong with getting a little assistance from this perfect specimen standing in front of her. It wasn't like she was going to fuck him. Hell, this was Vegas, and what happened in Vegas was going to stay right here between these four khaki-colored walls.

Payton gulped another swig of the champagne and scooted her hips to the edge of the table, never losing contact with his hand as he massaged her clit with just the right amount of pressure. She reached forward, grabbed a fistful of his shoulder-length blond hair, and guided his mouth to the intensity he'd ignited between her thighs. With every flick of his tongue, the pressure mounted in her core, and it wasn't long before the first wave, then the second wave hit. She tossed her head back, spiraling into the abyss of electric sensations zigzagging through her extremities.

"Shit," she cried out.

The room dipped and spun like a reckless carnival ride as tiny particles of pleasure flickered around her.

"Oh gawd, oh gawd, oh gawd!" she exhaled, totally lost in her senses.

Before she could catch her breath, her body still tingling, the technician stepped back, used the back of his hand to wipe her juices from his lips, and excused himself from the room.

In a postorgasmic haze, Payton sauntered toward the washbasin, but paused at her reflection in the full-length mirrors propped along the far wall. Medium height, with enough tits and ass to stop men in their tracks. Not bad for thirty-eight. Once she reached the sink, Payton noted her almond-brown eyes and flawless skin. Her cheeks flushed from the oxytocin release or maybe in her case dopamine—the hormone men released after an orgasm. She was all woman, but didn't understand the hang-ups many females had when it came to sex. This was the first time she'd gotten off at the hands and mouth of a complete stranger, but pleasure simply validated her existence. Nothing more, nothing less. Not that happily ever after bullshit most women are taught. Hell, a good head job always put a smile on her face and who wouldn't want that?

Out of the corner of her eye, a pink leather-bound stylebook labeled *Vajazzle Designs* caught her attention. She opened the book and began flipping through the pages, all the while remembering reading online about some celebrity who had put crystals on her vajayjay to get over a bad breakup. The elaborate designs were beautiful, but the thought of where all those tiny jewels could end up wasn't appealing. She lingered at the more-simple designs of a tiny heart and the butterfly silhouette that almost matched her tattoo. These were more than enough bling to cheer her up and enough sparkle for David to play Connect the Crystals later.

After freshening up, Payton returned to the suite to find a different technician waiting.

"Where's Marco?" she questioned.

The man extended his hand. "Hello, Ms. Jones. My name is

Samuel. I'll be finishing up your treatments. I promise to take good care of you. Marco had another appointment."

"I bet he does," Payton mumbled to herself.

She shared her design selection with Samuel and made her way to the waxing bed. Twenty minutes later he handed her a mirror to inspect his finished work.

She grinned. "Perfect."

Off-the-cuff surprises like this kept men guessing and were every woman's secret weapon. It kept the relationship fresh, mysterious, and men didn't know what to expect next, but Anthony "Tony" Barnes was the one man who seemed oblivious to her charms. He was single and the prime example of why Payton preferred to date married men.

A few weeks ago, he'd seen her in the front window of Pican's restaurant having dinner with David and had the audacity to be angry with her. She and Tony hadn't agreed to be exclusive; they weren't even in a relationship. As far as she was concerned, they were friends with benefits. So what was the big fucking deal?

Sex on the regular with a single man had never appealed to Payton. Usually, after a few good orgasms, the last thing on her mind was talking, spooning, or cuddling. What she craved most was to spread-eagle across her thousand-thread-count sheets and not have her limbs touched by anything living or breathing. With married men, Payton set the parameters of the relationship from the beginning, and she required full reign of the rules of engagement.

With Tony, things were different. He never crowded her space. But come to think of it, they always operated on *his* terms. They fucked when he wanted to, he came over when he wanted to—everything when he wanted to. Tony Barnes had somehow flipped her script and slithered his way under her skin. How the hell did she let that happen?

With her hidden bling in tow and a few designer shopping bags from her quick retail excursion, Payton made her way back to the Palms Hotel, much more relaxed than she'd been when she'd ventured out this morning. The hotel suite door barely closed behind her before her cell phone beeped and buzzed for the third time like it was possessed. From the designated ringtone, she knew exactly who the person blowing her phone up was—her uncle Sheldon. Payton paused for a moment, stared at the LCD screen in frustration, and laughed at the irony. During her early college years, Sheldon Jones spoiled her rotten. He held down a job at the local steel plant, sending her money and calling her weekly just to check in, but by the time her junior year rolled around, his calls began to lessen and eventually ceased, his addiction to crack cocaine the culprit. Back then, Payton would have done anything to hear her uncle's voice on the other end of a phone line. Now, since her grandparents' deaths and Sheldon's spiral into a drug-induced abyss, it was like taking care of a child. Always something. In her opinion, a grown-ass man needed to be fully responsible for his own life, her main motivation for selling her grandparents' house. She was exhausted and once she divided up the money from the sale of the house, there would be no reason for his frequent phone calls and foolishness. She placed the Louis Vuitton and Gucci bags on the table near the door and accepted the call.

"Hello."

"'Bout time you answered. I've been calling you for the last two hours."

Payton sighed heavily at his phantom sense of urgency. This man had such a flare for theatrics. "I'm out of town—"

"Out of town! Well, how am I gon' get my money?"

"Uncle Sheldon, quit being so dramatic. I'll be back in town tomorrow."

"Girl, didn't I tell you the last time I saw you I needed my money," he screamed into the phone.

"Have you given any thought to what we talked about the last time you saw me? When I get back in town tomorrow, we can go check out a few places."

"You sound just like your mama. And I'm telling you, just like I told her the other day, I ain't going to no damn rehab. I like to smoke crack. Besides, that shit don't work no way," he grumbled.

Payton fell silent. There it was again. First, a few weeks ago, the crazy girl who tried to kill Donathan and Sydney stopped by her grandparents' house looking for Lois Greene. Now, Sheldon mentioned the bitch who gave birth to her like the two of them were best friends and Lois lived right next door. Was this a coincidence? If it wasn't, why would this poor excuse for a mother come back to Pittsburg? Twenty-five years ago, Lois dropped a then-twelve-year-old Payton off at the movie theater, and that was the last time she'd seen or heard from her since. If her paternal grandparents hadn't taken her in, there was no telling how her life would have turned out.

Payton's thoughts grew dark. Was Sheldon trying to set her up? *Hell no*, she thought, laughing out loud. Sheldon Maurice Jones wasn't that smart, that deep, or that intentional.

"Are you laughing at me?"

"No, I'm crying for you," she said sharply. "Why won't you let me help you?"

"Girl, for the last time, I don't need no help! All I need from you is my money."

CHAPTER 2

Once Donathan James decided he wanted something, there was no turning back. And what he wanted most right now was for his wife to answer his goddamn question. Did she fuck Miles Day?

Trained eyes flickered past her cotton and lace camisole, then lingered on her exposed cocoa-brown skin, much more clothing than he preferred. The rise and fall of her shallow breaths and the tiny diamond navel ring that shone above the waist of her matching panties hypnotized him. His mind wrestled with the thought and his heart constricted in his chest at the possibility that she'd been with another man. Careful not to wake her, Donathan gently buried his nose in her freshly washed hair—inhaling deeply a familiar mixture of mint and lavender, something he always did, with no explanation.

Did she fuck Miles Day?

Everything about Sydney James was natural, feminine, and effortlessly beautiful. There was a glowing quality about her he could never get enough of. When he noticed the faint bruise on her brow, his anger seeped to the surface again.

With the pad of his thumb, Donathan gently brushed the fading contusion, she stirred, then shifted her weight to her side, her back now facing him. He inspected his almost-healed knuckles, his mind navigating the altercation and the past few weeks. To the naked eye, the physical reminders of the fight with Miles Day were almost gone, but the repercussions of what took place at the small, well-loved eatery weeks ago still echoed in his bed. There were many things he was sorry for that day, one being that during the exchange of blows with Miles, Sydney got tangled up in the crossfire and he accidentally struck her. He loved his woman with every breath in his body and would never intentionally strike her. Only cowards put their hands on women.

He couldn't believe the amount of damage they'd done to the place, and he was sorry for his role in that, but he wasn't sorry for kicking Miles Day's ass. He could see straight through the manipulative bastard. He knew the game all too well, hell a few times he'd been the shoulder to cry on himself. Miles had been laying the groundwork right under his nose for weeks, pretending to be Sydney's friend, when all along his ulterior motive was to get her in his bed. Women needed to understand that men were natural predators looking for an opportunity to pounce. If you let them hang around long enough, you would get fucked. Which is exactly what he was afraid of.

Sydney hadn't admitted to anything and wanted him to believe he'd overreacted when it came to Miles, but it was what Sydney hadn't said, what he wanted and needed to hear from her lips, that bothered him most. Who the hell did Miles think he was, telling him what not to do to his wife?

Some of his radio show fans witnessed the debacle, a marketing nightmare for his private practice and on-air presence, which resulted in the station suspending his morning "sex doctor" segments. But he didn't give a damn about any of that. The radio clips were how Austyn Greene had fixated on him in the first place. At least that's what she'd said when she arrived at the Richmond Country Club with every intention of luring him into her web, and like a damn fool he'd fallen for it. Should have listened to his gut instincts and run as far away from those ruby-red lips as he could. Then he wouldn't have ended up drugged, tied up in that hotel room—almost castrated.

★ ★ ★

When sleep finally overtook him, Donathan found himself back in Austyn Greene's apartment, drugged, paralyzed, and helpless. Her jet-black hair pulled taut into a ponytail exposing her exotic features taunted him—with the shiny scalpel gripped tightly in her hand. Austyn's words reverberated in his dream. *"You should have helped me and not tried to fuck me like all the others."*

Donathan woke in a cold sweat, disoriented, his heart beating fast, almost leaping out of his chest. He felt exposed and vulnerable. For several weeks he'd chewed sleeping pills like candy, but there weren't enough sleeping pills in the world that could help him tonight. Unfortunately for him, he'd underestimated Austyn, but he wouldn't get caught slipping like that again. In fact, there would be no rest for him until Austyn Greene was found and put away so she couldn't hurt anyone else.

Careful not to wake Sydney, Donathan eased out of bed and made his way down the spiral staircase into his home office. It was early, still dark but approaching dawn. On occasions when sleep eluded him, he used the quiet time to prep for his morning radio show segments or catch up on patient charting, but since neither of those activities were a part of his daily routine right now, there was nothing for him to do. Donathan caught a glimpse of his tired eyes and ashen skin on the twenty-seven-inch computer screen before he powered it on.

He felt like a fraud. A clinical psychologist, suffering from posttraumatic stress disorder, in desperate need of a psychologist of his own. He grunted at the irony. It was one thing to be covered in the veil of a cheating scandal—hell, cheating was something men did. But to be overpowered by a woman of that size twice left a bad taste in his mouth. People looked at him like he was weak. After mindlessly searching the internet awhile, Donathan found himself immersed in a dark-blue file folder. The outside of the folder was plain and inconspicuous, but a label bearing *Curtis Holsey, Investigations* was pasted on the inside pocket. He reread the contents for the umpteenth time, hopeful he'd find a clue to locate the troubled girl, tossed from one foster home to another.

Miraculously, during high school, Austyn Greene became an honor student and was accepted into UCLA, his and Sydney's alma mater, eventually landing in medical school of all places. This fact was mind-blowing to Donathan, but it explained her obvious familiarity with a scalpel.

Massaging the bridge of his nose, he leaned back into the leather office chair and sighed heavily. Some would read this information and praise how, through all the adversity and abuse this child had suffered, she'd made it out, but the therapist in him knew better. Austyn Greene had been a ticking time bomb for years, waiting for the right insult to explode. His instincts told him his paranoia wasn't a silly overreaction. Where the hell was she? Austyn's whereabouts were unknown, and the police search hadn't found anything useful. It was as if she'd just vanished into thin air.

Words she had spoken to him in her apartment echoed in his head again: *"I almost found her in Pittsburg, met somebody who kind of looked like her. Lois Greene is going to wish she had never been born. I am going to kill that bitch."*

He flipped the file pages with purpose, this time searching for anything he could find on Lois Greene. The dossier listed her last known address in Southern California, but the million-dollar question was whether she had Bay Area connections rooted in Pittsburg.

In all his years as a therapist he never understood how anyone could knowingly harm an innocent child. What type of woman would sell her daughter for a hit of crack cocaine? Donathan thought back to Austyn's account of the abuse. At the time he had no idea if she was lying or telling the truth. And even though she wasn't his patient, her confessions haunted him.

Psychologists were trained to get both sides of the story before drawing any type of conclusion, but in this case it was all about Austyn's perception, the driving force behind her need for revenge. The type of retaliation that would keep her here hunting for the target until Lois Greene got what Austyn felt she deserved. Austyn was still here—he could feel it.

Donathan located the business card for Curtis Holsey and hesitated. The private investigator had proven to be shady. He attempted to double-cross one of Donathan's closest friends, Tyrese, by extorting money from him to keep him from exposing his infidelity. Tyrese paid the ruthless investigator, which proved to be futile because his wife found out and left him anyway. Holsey didn't have any integrity and was clearly in it for the money.

Donathan typed "private investigator" into the Google search bar and a link for *The Best 10 Private Investigation Firms in Oakland, CA* popped up. He clicked, then scanned the list of investigators and chuckled to himself when he didn't find Holsey Investigations. None of the names on the list jumped out at him, and the thought of bringing someone new up to speed on the case gave him a sense of uneasiness. Last time, Holsey had been thorough and quick, which was exactly what Donathan needed right now. Finding and vetting a new investigator wasn't his top priority. Locating Austyn Greene was. He couldn't deny the dude was slick and couldn't be trusted, but it was Holsey's gutter mentality that would lead him right to where Austyn was hiding.

Without further hesitation, Donathan picked up the receiver and dialed the numbers displayed on the card. It was too early to reach Holsey, but he would feel better once he left a message. The phone rang once.

"Holsey."

Donathan was caught off guard when the live hoarse voice piped through the phone.

"Hello?" the raspy voice barked again.

"Sorry, man, I didn't expect you to answer your phone at five in the morning."

"I don't get paid to sleep. How can I help you, Dr. James?"

"How did you know it was me?" Donathan said, eyeing the private phone he used to phone patients from time to time that obviously wasn't as private as he believed.

"You have heard of caller ID, haven't you?"

"Yeah, I have, but AT&T assured me the number was private. I'm calling from a blocked number—"

"Dr. James, I make a living finding out things about people they don't want other people to know, like phone numbers for starters. Now, what can I do for you?"

"I have some more work for you."

"This wouldn't have anything to do with the story that's been leading the local news, would it?"

Donathan made his way to the office window, peeked out, then groaned. At some point something had to be done about the news hounds camped outside his front gate. Donathan thought that by him and Sydney not giving a statement, the story would quickly be dethroned as the Bay Area's hot topic, but over three weeks had passed, and even though the numbers dwindled, a handful of reporters were still there.

"I need your help finding her again."

"Aren't the police looking for her?"

"Yeah, but I don't know how much of a priority she is to them. This woman is a threat to my wife and my life. I need her found ASAP."

"Ya know, this new deal requires new money. I need a new retainer fee plus expenses and—"

"Your fee is not a problem."

"Well, since you have so much money to burn, cash is my preferred method of payment."

"I can meet with you later—"

Holsey cut him off. "Good. I'll get back to you with a location. In the meantime, you might want to just lie low and stay put behind that nice gate of yours. It sounds like you got a real loony tune on your hands. And in my experience, people like Austyn Greene don't usually go away until they get what they're looking for."

Donathan pondered that last statement a moment. Holsey was right. Like most victims of abuse, Austyn Greene suffered from low self-esteem and a distorted view of herself that made her susceptible to abusers. Usually, this was an accurate profile of such cases. Unlike Austyn, rarely did a subject do a complete 360-degree turnaround and go from being visibly troubled to a stellar member of society. She had become a medical doctor for Christ's sake, a task that even he, to his mother's chagrin, had been unable to master. But every once in a while, abuse victims became sociopaths, their pain the driving force behind their destructive behaviors. Austyn Greene was both. And although he and Sydney were locked in her crosshairs, there was someone else she wanted more. Austyn believed one woman was to blame for the current state of her life, and she would stop at nothing until she made her pay.

"Holsey, change of plans. I need you to locate someone else for me."

"Who's that?"

"Austyn's mother. I need you to help me find Lois Greene."

CHAPTER 3

Austyn Greene's pulse quickened, her thoughts in overdrive and agitated by the loud noises jarring through the poorly insulated Sheetrock. She hobbled unevenly to the door to check the lock operated from the inside by a thumb turn, then latched the safety chain for added protection. She didn't know how much longer she could survive in this hellhole, yet she was out of options at the moment.

The roadside motel was a haven for drug addicts, sexual deviants, and gum-chewing prostitutes—a dump by anyone's standards. The pain in her right knee pounded in sync with the elevated voices as she limped away from the door, to switch on the bedside lamp resting on the side table. Her hands shook as she reached for her backpack, opened the bottle of painkillers, and managed to pop a few in her mouth, before chasing them down with the half-empty bottle of water on the nightstand.

Austyn inspected the bruise where the steel lever made impact with her kneecap. She couldn't believe she let that bitch, Sydney James, do this to her.

Over the past few weeks, the swelling had gone down considerably, but the constant ache hadn't ceased. Austyn leaned back against the faux-wood headboard and fixated on a single spot of peeling paint on the ceiling.

Attempting to silence the chaos, she plugged her ears with her two middle fingers and hummed out loud. When she'd stopped at this roadside motel a few weeks ago and paid cash to rent a room for a month, the manager on duty took the payment, gave her a key, and never asked any questions. It was her just-in-case option. She had no intention of ever using the dingy space until she found Donathan James snooping through her apartment, then it became her only option.

Austyn grinned, recalling the look on Donathan's face when she stabbed him in the neck with the loaded syringe and watched his full height buckle to the floor. But then everything went completely wrong. One minute she was about to give Donathan James just what he deserved; the next minute his wife, Sydney, busted her knee with a tire iron and loud sirens had her on the run. By the time she reached the old car she kept stashed around the corner—her plan B—she was barefoot and blinded by fury, and her knee had ballooned to the size of a small melon. She had to get away from there . . . to be safe. Austyn retrieved the spare key attached to the underside of the car bumper, then drove to the very place that was now her prison—Pittsburg.

"Dammit," she gasped, as a sharp pain sliced through her knee. She reached for the almost-empty water bottle and flung it across the room.

"Shut the fuck up!" she screamed at the wall. "I should have killed them both when I had the chance."

Did Donathan remember her rant about Pittsburg?

Of course not, the voice in her head assured her.

Her mind's eye replayed the reel of Donathan James sprawled across her living room floor, intoxicated by the effects of the drug and drifting in and out of consciousness. There was no way he could remember the things she'd said to him. All the things she'd shared with him that day were their little secret.

"Hmph," she barked at the irony.

For years she drowned in secrets. Her breath quickened at the thought of the rapes, the beatings, then hitched in her throat at the memory of being fondled by random men at the direction of her mother. When she heard Donathan James on the radio show giving information and bragging about how he helped his patients, she thought he was different, thought he could help her, but he turned out to be just like all the others.

Consumed by the hunger for revenge, a sudden rush of anger made its way to the surface of her mind as she moved toward the air-conditioning unit affixed to the wall. If the sex doctor did tell the police, she didn't have much time before they came looking for her.

"Fuck!" Austyn winced, panting through the pain as she eased her way to the floor, then untapped a Phillips head screwdriver from the bottom panel.

Getting tossed into a jail cell was not on her agenda. Not before she located Lois Greene, the bitch who put this avalanche in motion, and not before she made Donathan and Sydney James pay.

Austyn removed the front panel of the cooling unit and retrieved a small black case no bigger than the size of a small cosmetic bag. The woman's screams and the crashing of what sounded like drawers opening and closing, being pulled from the plywood dresser and tossed to the ground, sent Austyn's heart rate into overdrive again. She scooted closer to the wall, leaned in, and listened. She flinched with every slap, as if she could feel the palm-to-skin contact coming from the other side of the plaster wall.

"Bitch, you've been working all day, and this is all the money you have? You must be skimming or fucking for free," the man yelled before he struck the girl again.

"Ray, please don't," the girl begged. "I swear I didn't take no money."

The room grew quiet before her barely audible sobs intensified.

"Well, somebody been sleeping on the job, 'cause you should be an expert at what to do with that mouth and the heat between your legs. Get your ass over here and let daddy give you a lesson."

A few minutes passed, but it wasn't long before deep moans

and grunts smothered the room. Austyn sat paralyzed as the constant thud of the headboard flooded her mind with images of the
filthy man who'd stolen her innocence. Bile rose in her throat as she
relived the first time. Her body crushed by the weight of the grown
man lying on top of her. He played with her almost-budding
breasts, before it quickly escalated into something much worse. Lois
looked on, unfazed by Austyn's tears.

Lois said, "Shush, girl. It's only going to hurt this one time.
Now stop all this foolishness so the man can finish his business."

Austyn's body trembled uncontrollably, then drifted into a
back-and-forth rocking synchronized with the hard and steady
rhythm of the headboard as it banged against the wall. Her movements stopped abruptly. She unzipped the black toiletry bag she
had retrieved from the air-conditioning unit, removed the scalpels,
syringes, and vials of medication, then placed them one by one on
the worn brown carpet next to her. The banging grew louder and
faster, followed by the howl-like moans signifying the predator
had finished his business. Austyn became eerily calm, hypnotized
by the bedside light bouncing off the surgical instruments.

"They all have to pay," she murmured through her posttraumatic haze, knowing that Lois Greene's debt was immeasur-
able and way overdue.

CHAPTER 4

"Open and close your hand for me," the surgeon said, examining the wound and what was left of a few sutures on Sydney James's right hand.

Sydney did as instructed. With each opening and closing, the palm of her hand tightened, then relaxed. Flashes of her altercation with Austyn Greene invaded her thoughts. It was as if she could feel the scalpel as it sliced through her palm.

The sharp surgical instrument cut clean, but when the paramedics arrived, her blood was everywhere, including all over Donathan. The hand surgeon reached for the magnifying lamp affixed to the wall, continuing his extensive scrutiny for what seemed like an eternity. He made eye contact.

"I'm very pleased with your progress, Dr. James. There's no sign of infection, and the cut is healing nicely. I'd like to refer you to a few sessions of heat therapy, then you should be good as new."

Sydney raised an eyebrow. "Heat therapy? How long will that take?"

The doctor smiled, then shook his head. "Doctors make the worst patients. Remember, it's your dominant surgical hand, Dr. James," he said, brushing his finger along the scar line. "Your hand needs to be better than new. Heat therapy will reduce any internal inflammation, further stimulate the healing process, and lessen the buildup of scar tissue."

"When can I go back to work?"

"Let's give it another three weeks."

"Three weeks! You can't be serious," she blurted out.

There was no way in hell she could take another day, much less three whole weeks, cooped up in the house with Donathan. His withdrawn, moody, and unpredictable behavior drove her crazy. Before Miles Day, sex had never been a problem in their relationship. She and Donathan could touch, tease, and taste one another all day long without either growing tired, but something had clearly changed. One minute he treated her like a breakable doll, waiting on her hand and foot; the next they screwed like jackrabbits. It seemed like he was in the midst of an invisible competition, with something to prove—and determined to fuck her senseless.

The doctor interrupted her internal pity party.

"Here's the deal. I will allow you back into the hospital on light duty, if—"

"I promise to do whatever you say, Dr. Lawrence."

"No surgery yet, and once you complete the physical therapy, I'll need to take one more look at your hand before I release you completely, without modifications."

"Thank you, Jesus," she said, her voice trailing off.

"My assistant will schedule another appointment for you for about four weeks out, and I'll also have her draw up the work release forms. Take them to your employer, and I'm sure they'll have you back on the hospital schedule before you leave the building."

The hand surgeon turned to exit the room, but stopped short when he reached the door. He pivoted to face her. "Dr. James, I can't tell you how lucky you are. The cut was clean and left minimal nerve damage. A half of an inch deeper, and there would have been some serious implications for your surgical career."

The door to the exam room swung closed, and Sydney waited in silence. Over the past few weeks she, too, had wondered *what if* a thousand times. What if Austyn Greene had severed the nerves in her dominant hand? What she saw when she arrived at Austyn's apartment would be forever etched in her memory. A paralyzed Donathan sprawled unnaturally across the floor and a crazy woman wielding a carbon steel surgical blade. If she hadn't intervened when she did, Donathan would have been the latest victim in Austyn Greene's string of unthinkable crimes . . . he might even be dead. If she had to do it all over again, she wouldn't change a thing, even if the outcome had been catastrophic for her.

After what seemed like a never-ending lecture on all the things she couldn't do, Sydney left the doctor's office with her paperwork in hand and made a beeline straight to Children's Hospital. By the time she turned into the doctors' parking lot, her nerves were frayed. She'd been so eager to turn in the release paperwork so she could get back to her patients, she hadn't thought this all the way through. What would it be like facing her coworkers after they witnessed the Lois-the-Pie-Queen showdown between Miles and Donathan? Not to mention her husband being the lead story on most of the Bay Area news outlets over the past few weeks.

The anxiety in her gut bubbled as she picked up the doctor's release off the passenger seat and made her way inside the building. On the elevator ride up to the HR department, Sydney fidgeted, searching her mind for a recent memory of the last time she'd seen a patient. The sweet little girl who'd been viciously attacked by the neighbor's dogs came to mind. The child had been given a diagnosis of never being able to walk again, but the last time Sydney examined her, the little girl used a walker to take her first steps. Sydney sighed heavily. If only her personal life wasn't so complicated. The situation with Donathan made her joy of practicing medicine come with a heavy dose of shame and embarrassment.

"C'mon, girl, you can do this," she muttered before stepping off the elevator.

She had to take back control of her life, but her game plan for now was to drop the paperwork off to Human Resources and make it back to her car without talking to anybody. She thought about Miles, and guilt rose in the pit of her belly. He hadn't returned any of her phone calls, which was surprising. Over the past few months, he had been there for her during her marital troubles in ways her closest friends weren't. The last time she saw him, he and Donathan were exchanging blows, and she had yet to confirm from Miles himself that he was okay. After all, she was the reason they were fighting in the first place.

"Sydney?"

The sound of her name oozed through the air like a snake slithering across the floor. Sydney continued to maneuver the maze of hallways toward Human Resources, pretending not to hear the voice, although she did. Of all the people she could have encountered today, why did it have to be Julia Stevens's trouble-making ass?

"Sydney James?" she called again in a high-pitched voice. "Oh my goodness! Is it you?"

Sydney stopped, turned around, and faced the false epitome of perfection. Full-face makeup, designer attire, not a single strand of fiery-red hair out of place. Even her lab coat fit her like it had been custom-tailored.

"You were the last person I expected to see up here."

Julia Stevens was a rail-thin woman, and if her attitude wasn't so nasty, she could be considered pretty in a rigid sort of way. She hailed from Boston, the daughter of a very wealthy businessman, and at every turn she made sure everyone was well aware of that fact.

"Why is that? I do work here."

"Well, I mean you've been missing in action for weeks, and after that little fiasco at Lois the Pie Queen and that other situation, I don't blame you." Julia leaned in close and lowered her voice. "People have been whispering, if you know what I mean. Especially with you and Miles both being MIA at the same time. I keep telling him it's time to get back to work."

Sydney's heart constricted. If Miles wasn't working, where

was he? Did Donathan hurt him? Was he okay? Returning to work definitely wasn't as appealing as it had been a few hours ago. She didn't know if she could tolerate daily encounters like this with Julia and the stares and whispers from her colleagues. But work was the one constant in her life that could keep her sane right now.

"Excuse me, but are we watching the same news? The stations I watch have been very clear that my husband and I were both victims of a vicious crime, so there's nothing to whisper about."

Sydney's eyes found her feet. She knew that was a lie before she finished the sentence. The news stations had been brutal and muddy. In fact, a few outlets were still camped outside her home, impeding her comings and goings. They wanted Donathan's side of the story, but up until now, he'd refused to say a single word.

"That's all fine and dandy, but that doesn't stop hospital gossip." Julia reached for her hand, but Sydney jerked it away. "How's the hand?"

"Not that it's any of your business, but my hand is fine."

"No need to get testy," Julia said with a feeble chuckle.

The two stared at each other in silence for a moment, then Julia continued, "Well, I'm due in surgery. We'll continue this little chat at another time. Toodles."

Julia hurried off, and Sydney stood frozen, staring at the white lab coat flapping behind her. She couldn't believe the nerve of that red-haired bitch pretending to be concerned about her well-being. She knew Julia was the ringleader of all the gossip and whispers. This was a clear indication of the type of harassment to come. She made her way to HR and turned in the paperwork, all the while questioning in her mind what she was going to do about it.

Feeling sorry for herself, Sydney hurried home, only to be greeted by the paparazzi posted at the front gate.

"Shit," she cursed under her breath. Something had to be done about this craziness. When Donathan got home this evening, they were going to talk. They needed another plan to get these reporters to stop acting like vultures circling a carcass.

Once inside, Sydney kicked off her shoes and stopped off at the wine cellar to grab a bottle of LVE, an exclusive collection from the singer John Legend before making her way to the kitchen. She couldn't get the bottle of Chardonnay uncorked fast enough to savor the buttery flavors. Her tolerance for alcohol told her not to have more than one glass, but taking large gulps she quickly downed two and immediately felt light-headed.

Tonight she refused to eat another meal from a to-go container. The bandages were off, and Donathan wasn't home to nag her about overdoing it. Still holding her wineglass, Sydney opened the refrigerator to survey the contents. Recyclable takeout containers covered every shelf, evidence of life at the James's residence the past few weeks. Her cell phone chirped, and anxiety rose in her throat as she peered into her almost-empty glass before she remembered she was off work. When she fished the handset out of her purse, a text from Donathan was displayed on the screen.

Are you home? Meeting Tony for dinner and drinks.

Sydney placed the wineglass on the counter and tried to type with two thumbs, but the pull in the center of her right hand turned her words to gibberish. She backspaced feverishly and settled on one word.

Yes.

She stared at the device, awaiting his response.

Miss Ollie's. Want something?

Sydney's mouth watered at the thought of Miss Ollie's fried chicken, seasonal greens, and garlic-oil-fried plantains, but if a good meal meant she'd have to wait up and possibly encounter one of his foul moods, she would pass. This time she used her pointer finger to respond.

No. I'm fine.

Are you sure? I can send you something via UberEats . . .

Sydney ruminated on the offer briefly, then quickly abandoned the thought. The wait time didn't appeal to her. She wanted something quick and something she prepared with her own two hands. She typed.

I'm good. Enjoy your time with Tony.

Beginning to feel the slight buzz, Sydney relinquished her wineglass, laid the phone down on the granite counter, grabbed a few eggs, and whipped up a cheese omelet in no time. Another glass of wine, a hot bath, and one of her mindless reality TV shows was just what the doctor ordered. If she were lucky, maybe Donathan would have a drink or two himself and relax. Maybe then he would come home and actually make love to her like he used to instead of pressing her about Miles.

CHAPTER 5

Anthony Barnes aka Tony entered the standing-room-only crowd at Liege Spirits Lounge, a popular hangout spot in downtown Oakland. He moved through the mob of people standing shoulder to shoulder until he found Donathan perched at the bar, deep in conversation with an exotic beauty. The scene reminded Tony of the time at the Richmond Country Club when he'd found his best friend deep in conversation with the crazy bitch who had tried to kill him. The two women looked nothing alike. This one appeared to be in her late twenties, short build, looked half Puerto Rican and half something else. He watched her lean into Donathan's personal space, hanging on his every word. She batted her lashes, giggled on cue, and arched her back, making sure his free hand made contact with her perfectly round ass. This chick looked good, but Tony didn't understand how Donathan could be so comfortable with this woman after his recent ordeal. Yeah, that ass was juicy, but as far as he was concerned, nobody could be trusted. Everybody was a suspect.

Without making eye contact, Donathan removed his suit jacket from the bar stool next to him, and Tony took the seat. He couldn't help wondering how he and Donathan, best friends since the age of ten, could be so close, yet as opposite as night and day when it came to women. From the time girls entered the picture,

Donathan always had to have more than one. Tony, on the other hand, was single and believed in monogamous relationships. Yet despite their differences, Tony knew that no matter the circumstances, they would always have each other's backs. Donathan raised his voice to be heard.

"What happened to you texting me when you made it down here?"

Tony picked up Donathan's cell phone off the bar and held it up to display the multiple unanswered text messages. "I did."

After Tony downed a few beers, they walked less than a block to Miss Ollie's, the Caribbean soul food restaurant perched between Ninth and Tenth streets in Old Town Oakland. On a Friday night, this intersection transformed into a constant hum of cell phone conversations and people socializing on the streets while waiting for a coveted open seat at one of the establishments on each of the four corners.

"I'll be right back," Donathan said, after they stepped inside the restaurant. He trotted off through an open door with a sign that read *Restrooms*.

"Do you have a reservation?" the male greeter asked. "The wait time is over forty-five minutes if you don't—"

"Last name James," Tony replied, eliminating the need for the young man to continue the rote dialogue he'd been serving up to anyone who stepped up to the wood podium with a request for dinner seating.

The restaurant was crowded with most of the tables taken, but Tony was escorted to a table with a clear view of Washington Street, prime real estate on a Friday evening.

But for him socializing wasn't a priority. Since his mother's death due to stage-four breast cancer, he'd become the sole caretaker of his fifteen-year-old sister, Najee. And he had no clue what he was doing. It was summertime, and next week he was due back at work. A babysitter was out of the question, and according to

Najee she was way too old for any type of camp. What the hell was he going to do with her?

He reflected back on how his mother, Shirley Barnes—a single mother—had single-handedly given him the very best of herself, all while working multiple jobs to keep a roof over their heads. He prayed he could do the same for his little sister. He grinned at the memory of that evening almost sixteen years ago when Shirley told him she was going to have a baby. At the time, he couldn't believe his mother was having sex, let alone a baby at forty-three. Tony shook his head at the irony. Now he was forty-two years old, and although he wasn't anybody's baby daddy, he was horny as hell, and therein lay the problem.

Even though he wasn't the type of brother who lied to women or had multiple partners running through his house, there were a few regulars he visited from time to time. It had only been a month, but this new living situation had put a tremendous strain on his sex life. He couldn't make a call on a whim or stay out all night anymore without making plans for the whereabouts of his sister. But to be honest, not getting laid wasn't really about Najee or his mother.

Payton Marie Jones was the true culprit.

For the past six months, he had only been having sex with Payton, and in the end her lying and deceitful ass turned out to be his worst nightmare.

"Damn, is it that bad?" Donathan said lightly before easing himself into the seat across from Tony.

"What?" Tony said sharply.

"Bro, the frown etched across your forehead is rippling."

The waiter appeared, delivering two highball glasses filled with a two-toned concoction decorated with cherries, pineapple, and a lime wedge on the rim, along with a shot of bourbon. "Keep the bourbon coming," Donathan said. He raised his glass and waited for Tony to do the same.

"Man, what is this, and when did you start drinking?"

"Can't come to Miss Ollie's and not do the rum punch. Here's to a night off and permission to feel no pain."

"Well, I'm glad you had sense enough to know I needed something just a little stronger than this." Tony raised both glasses, downed the fruity mixture, and chased it with the brown liquid. He winced at the burn at the back of his throat. Bourbon was meant to be sipped slowly, but that wouldn't be the case tonight. He placed the empty glass on the table and signaled to the waiter for another drink.

"Man, I could drink until I'm blue in the face, which would be hard to do, but this hole in my chest ain't going anywhere—"

"Of course it isn't," Donathan admonished. "Your mom was sick for a long time, but what's wrong with a little temporary happiness? I mean, take a serious look out the window."

Tony scanned the droves of thirty-something professional women heading toward the District Wine and Whiskey Lounge. Donathan was right. He was in dire need of a little temporary happiness. He made eye contact with the woman ogling him from outside the window, but the reality of his newfound responsibilities killed that buzz in an instant. Even if he and the woman agreed on the rules of engagement, he didn't have a lot of time, and taking her to his house was definitely out of the question.

Tony fell back into the high-backed bench and let out a deep sigh. His aunt Rosemary was home with Najee tonight, but tomorrow she was heading back to Texas, and he still hadn't figured out what he was going to do. He'd gone from living the life of a bachelor to having to move his mother and sister into his house with him. And now that his mother was gone, overnight he'd become the legal guardian of his sister—no longer responsible for just himself.

"Man, I'm not like you. Temporary happiness scares the shit out of me, and thanks to Austyn Greene, your ass should be terrified, too," Tony warned, then felt immediate remorse for bringing up that situation.

He'd been tempted to scold Donathan when they left Liege, but thought better of it. He couldn't get that crazy woman and what happened to his friend out of his mind. In fact, when he and Donathan were leaving the club, he could have sworn he'd seen a woman who looked like Austyn, except she had long blond braids.

His cell phone buzzed, and he quickly glanced at the screen. He swiped the glass to clear the message. Why the hell did Payton keep texting him? Her name alone conjured up the image of her with a man's fingers stuffed into her mouth, and he felt wounded all over again. The phone vibrated again, then again, and each time Tony swiped the screen to make the words vanish.

"Is Najee okay?"

"She's fine."

"Do we need to cut this short so you can handle that?" Donathan motioned toward the phone.

Tony's body language shifted. "Man, *that's* yesterday's news," he mumbled.

"A dose of yesterday's news might be just what you need right now—"

"Quit playing like you don't know," Tony snapped. "I know Sydney told you."

"Told me what?" Donathan said, his face now twisted in confusion.

Tony hesitated a moment, before he said, "Payton and I had a thing, but like I said, she's yesterday's news."

Donathan leaned back in his chair, processing this new information. "Excuse me, but did you just tell me you were fucking Payton?"

"Yeah."

"And Sydney knew about this?"

"She found out that night those pictures of you and Austyn were posted on the internet. Man, look. It's really not a big deal. I mean it's pretty obvious what it was . . ."

"Not as obvious as you seem to think it is. Two single people sneaking around like cheating married people. It doesn't make sense."

"We weren't sneaking around. Just two consenting adults, without expectations, having a good time."

"Really?" Donathan said. "Then why the secret?"

Tony mulled over the question a few minutes before he replied. "Because of this reaction I'm getting from you and the one we both got from Sydney. We wanted the situation to be defined by us—no outside pressure to make it more than it was."

"Okay, I get that, but what about now? Bring me up to speed on why she's blowing up your cell, and why you're ignoring her?"

Tony picked up the whiskey glass, sniffed the contents, and gulped it down in one shot.

He cleared his throat. "Bottom line—I was fucking her exclusively, but as it turns out, I'm the only one who got the memo."

"Did you just use Payton and the word 'exclusive' in the same sentence? I know she didn't agree to that."

Tony grew quiet as he contemplated Donathan's question. No, Payton hadn't agreed to any such thing.

"C'mon, man, you're killing me. You know better than that."

"Man, it just happened. Chalk it up to a lapse in judgment—a normal progression."

"Under normal circumstances, I would agree, but Payton is not normal."

Tony laughed, easing the sudden tension. He really didn't know what to say. Outside of the calls that ended in nasty exchanges, Tony had not really addressed the status of his relationship with Payton. She was texting him like crazy right now, and she'd called him a few times, but he had refused to return her texts or calls. The truth of the matter was, he'd fucked up.

He'd let his guard down during his mother's illness, had let Payton become more than a place for release. Idiosyncrasies and all, she'd become a place of comfort for him, and he thought they were better than her letting another man hand-feed her in public.

The phone vibrated again, and this time he read the message. *I really need to talk to you . . . I need to see you . . .*

His groin tightened, and a smug smile played at the corners of his mouth. His mind said, *Hell, fucking no*, but his body begged him to make a quick detour to Lakeside Drive, barge into Payton's apartment, and fuck her like she needed to be fucked. He wanted to yank her hair, palm her ass, and feel the things she did to him with her tongue. But she'd made him look like a fool, and he wasn't going out like that. The waiter replaced his drink, and Tony slid his phone across the table in Donathan's direction before downing another gulp of bourbon.

"Sounds like an invitation to me. Why don't you text her back? Both of you—"

"Hell no! I'm not texting or calling her ass back."

"Calm down." Donathan chuckled. "All I'm saying is, you could use a little stress relief right now, and that right there seems like the easiest place to get it."

CHAPTER 6

Payton Marie Jones barely made it through the X-ray machine before the female TSA agent accosted her. The aggressive touching began below Payton's armpits, brushing her breasts and trailing down both sides of her body, before a quick pat to her midsection.

"Wait a minute! What the hell are you doing?" Payton screamed, clutching her chest with her hands. She was wearing a thin cotton T-shirt dress, which gave her body very little protection.

"Ma'am, next time you can request to do this in private."

"Do what in private?" Payton said, her eyes narrowing to slits. "You've already felt on my tits and practically squeezed my ass. You should warn people before you start copping your feels."

The TSA agent turned beet red, clearly embarrassed by the remarks. "Ma'am, I'm just trying to do my job—"

"Your job does not give you the right to put your hands on me without permission. I don't believe this shit!" she said, scanning the crowd, surprised to see David Bryant a few passengers back waiting to pass through the X-ray machine. Why hadn't she seen him before now? His dark brown eyes locked with hers and sent intense searing heat into her before he slowly looked away. He didn't utter a single word, but she knew what he was thinking. How much he detested it when she made scenes in public. Payton took a deep breath.

"Are you done with this pat down?"

The TSA agent moved aside, and Payton stepped around the burly, handsome woman, then quickly collected her things from the conveyor belt. When she pivoted, David was standing within inches, his six-foot frame towering over her. Blistering eyes, broad shoulders, and close-cropped hair with hints of salt and pepper peeking at his temples. His perfect lips drove women crazy. And even though this man was incredibly handsome, it wasn't necessarily about his looks or the power that seeped from his pores. David had that "it" factor, and he knew it. He winked at her.

"Hmph," Payton grunted, clutched her belongings, and defiantly made her way toward the gate.

Screwing a powerful businessman definitely had its perks. David owned several Bay Area automotive dealerships, including a Mercedes one. He'd offered her a cute little coupe—on the house, of course—but Payton knew better than to accept a gift of that magnitude. If she took the car, David would think he owned her, and she was the type of woman who had always done things her way. She planned to keep doing just that.

During the two years they'd been friends, she'd traveled with him on numerous occasions with David's special code of conduct. No checking in together, unnecessary chitchat, or sitting together on the plane—crazy-ass rules. As far as David was concerned, on business trips their time together stopped before they exited the hotel room, which never quite made sense to Payton.

In Oakland, he wined and dined her out in the open, but for some reason business trips and airports were off-limits. In the beginning, Payton was fixated on this behavior and questioned David about it every chance she got. His response was some jargon about respect for his wife, which was a huge oxymoron coming from a married man who was cheating in the first place. But in the end, as long as Payton was in first class, too, she didn't give a damn if she sat next to David Bryant or not.

She thought back to him feeding her in public at Pican's a few weeks earlier. This display of intimacy had pissed Tony the hell off. In fact, he still wasn't accepting her calls or returning her texts.

David cleared his throat. Payton met his gaze head-on, her mind racing in a hundred different directions, none of them pleasant.

"What?" she hissed.

David grinned, shook his head, and took a seat next to her.

"What the hell are you doing?" she mouthed.

"Relax and breathe, Payton. Just breathe."

The flight to San Francisco was uneventful. By the time the car service made it across the Bay Bridge and dropped her off at her condo, Payton decided to head toward Pittsburg. As far as she was concerned, Highway 4 was one of the worst commutes in the country, and on her final day off, she wanted no part of that. It was barely 10 a.m., and since it was only a thirty-five-minute drive, she had plenty of time to stop by the bank, locate her wayward uncle Sheldon, and make it back to Oakland before rush-hour traffic.

Adrian Marcel's soulful serenade wafted through the sound system as Payton quickly fell into a driving rhythm. She prayed her uncle Sheldon was sober today and that she wouldn't get wrapped up in any of his nonsense. It seemed like the older her uncle got, the more ridiculous and exaggerated the drama in his life became. Who was she kidding? This was not about old age at all. It was his addiction to crack cocaine that kept his life in chaos. But lately, who was she to judge? She thought about the way her own life had been going over the last few months, and she still couldn't believe she'd allowed Sydney to talk her into that online dating fiasco. What the hell was she thinking? Luckily, she'd had sense enough to follow through on the date minimum requirement and received a full refund. But lately it seemed like every time they got together, their conversation focused on why Payton preferred to date married men. Sydney pleaded with her on more than one occasion to "stop dating other people's husbands." But that was easier said than done. She'd tried the non-attached-man thing with Tony and look where that got her.

When she took the Railroad exit, she dialed the number she

had for Sheldon again with no answer. She snickered at the irony. Yesterday, he blew up her cell phone repeatedly, and today her calls were the ones being sent to voice mail. She sat at the red light and pondered her next move. Sheldon didn't have a car, and the last time she saw him, he was riding a gray ten-speed bicycle. Pittsburg wasn't that big, but he could be anywhere.

As if it had a mind of its own, the midnight-blue Lexus drove toward Tenth Street and made its way to the familiar address. The ink on the contract finalizing the sale of the property was barely dry, but when she pulled alongside the curb in front of the house, a *Sold* sign was already staked in the front yard. The tri-level single-family home looked sad and lonely, no longer the place she grew up in. Soon after her father died, her drug-addicted mother abandoned her, and this house became her solace. Apart from her grandparents, her uncles Sheldon and Donald vowed to spoil her rotten and they did.

Payton was devastated when she returned from college at UCLA to find not one, but both of her uncles strung out on crack cocaine. This broke her grandparents' heart. And once her grandparents died, both men became her cross to bear.

Before she sold the house, she was practically living in Pittsburg, managing their mess. The brothers were fraternal twins, and Sheldon Jones was more than enough trouble for the both of them. Currently, Donald was in jail on a probation violation. Aside from him leaving a woman by the name of Sonya Mitchell to squat in the basement, he had the milder temperament of the two.

Just when she thought she'd have to delay the sale of the house to evict Sonya Mitchell in civil court, the woman had been caught passing bad checks at a department store in Antioch and sent to jail. Payton was so grateful when Detective McGrady, the police officer assigned to the case, informed her that Sonya Mitchell would be in jail long enough to sell the property without further incident.

A few weeks ago, she'd been so fed up with all of her uncles' shenanigans she thought once she sold the house and gave them their share of the inheritance from the sale, she would wash her hands of the situation. But now that it was done, she found herself torn. There was no way in her right mind she could give each of them $75,000 cash to end up in the hands of the local dope man. Her cell phone rang.

"Where are you?" Payton asked, relieved that Sheldon had finally returned her call.

"Heeeeyyyy, how is my number-one niecy?" he sang, sounding like he'd just won the lottery.

"Are you alright? Why aren't you answering your phone?"

"I'm a busy man, got things to do."

"Well, I'm busy, too. I told you I'd be out here today," she snapped.

"Girl, calm down. I'm right up the street. Meet me in the parking lot of the courthouse."

"The courthouse? Why didn't you tell me Uncle Donald had a court date?"

"Who said anything about Donald? I was up here supporting a friend who had to go to court today, and it's a damn shame they made that girl go to rehab for thirty days. If she wanted to get cleaned up, she'd go to rehab by her damn self."

Payton laughed. She guessed crackheads had friends, too. Then she pounced on the opportunity. "So why won't *you* get clean?"

"Girl, don't start with me this morning," he said irritably. "Just come on up here and give me my money. They holding me a spot at the Mar Ray Motel, and I need to check in before they run out of rooms."

"Why don't I just meet you at the motel? I can pay for a long-term rental for you," Payton said. The rush of the realization of what selling the house meant finally hit her. Both her uncles were now homeless, and it was all her doing. But as executor of the estate, she had to do something. The exposed wires, ripped-up carpet, and trash everywhere pushed her over the edge. Her choice was simple. Keep the house and let Sheldon burn it to the ground, or be fair and make sure they all got their financial share.

Payton hung up the phone and drove toward the motel, passing shells of people wandering around the sidewalks. Once word got around that Sheldon had money, fake friends and acquaintances would be eager to help him spend it. And unfortunately, Sheldon didn't have a discerning bone in his body. She looked to the heavens and shook her head. He wasn't going to like it, but she couldn't in good conscience give him full access to that kind of money. She just couldn't.

CHAPTER 7

When Donathan entered his office through the side door, he overheard Elaine, his secretary, on the phone.

"I'm sorry, but Dr. James is not available for interviews at this time. Would you like to leave a callback number?"

From the commotion outside, and the word "interview," he assumed it was a reporter. Not a flicker of judgment crossed her mocha-almond face as she handed him the newspaper.

"Thank you," he murmured.

Elaine Bates had been his secretary for well over ten years. She was organized, efficient, and somehow always knew exactly what to do without him saying a word. He unfolded the paper, witnessed the picture of him splashed across the cover, then made his way to his office. He was sick and tired of being the most sought-after story in the Bay Area. The blog chatter and local newspapers were out of control, some saying the "Sex Doctor" got what he deserved. Days passed, and reporters still camped outside his home, followed him wherever he went, hounding him for a story, and now they were at his office.

He closed the door, eased behind his desk, and stretched his long legs, as if settling in for a while. He needed the craziness to stop. The media had become such a circus that he felt it was in the best interest of his patients for him to cancel appointments and refer those who needed it to some of his colleagues for the next few weeks.

He opened the newspaper for a closer inspection and read the headline.

Suspect Drugs and Castrates Victims

Three men are dead after witnesses say they were last seen with a beautiful young woman. Police suspect this is the same woman who allegedly terrorized radio personality Dr. Donathan James.

He balled up the paper and sailed it across the room.

"Dammit, this story just won't die," he mumbled.

Donathan knew he wouldn't be able to keep this from his parents much longer. Maurice and Sylver James had returned home from a monthlong vacation in Europe last night. Although he had spoken to his parents several times since the incident, Donathan believed the situation would blow over before they were back on American soil. Now there would be hell to pay if they caught a glimpse of him on the news or read this article in today's paper without warning.

His mother, the prim and proper Sylver Monet James, was mortified when Donathan ditched medical school to pursue a doctorate in psychology instead of following in the footsteps of his highly acclaimed father, the cardiac surgeon. And all hell broke loose when he took the radio show gig. She couldn't understand why her son, who'd been afforded all the best opportunities in life, would stoop so low as to talk about sex on a live radio show.

Of course, he didn't see it that way. In college, once he took his first psychology class, he knew what his lifelong work would be. The science and theory of the human psyche intrigued him. And the radio show afforded him the opportunity to share a few theories with the masses, but to his irritation, it also made him a local superstar.

Handsome celebrity. A serial killer. Sex. Castration. Who was he kidding? Hell yeah! This had all the elements of continuous juicy headlines for weeks to come. His private line rang. "Shit," he grumbled after glancing at the caller ID. It was his mother.

Bad news didn't waste any time spreading, but he wasn't ready to talk to her right now, hadn't quite flushed out what he was going to say. If he lied and told her he had a patient, he could hurry her off the phone. But if he didn't speak with her, Sylver James would show up on his doorstep next, and with all the paparazzi that situation would be much worse. On the fourth and final ring, before the call went to voice mail, he picked up.

"Mom, can I call you back? My next patient—"

"Donathan Maurice James! I don't give a hoot about your patients. Have you seen the paper this morning? What in the world is going on over there?"

"Mom, I know I should have told you, but I didn't want to ruin your vacation."

"I don't care where I am in the world. If something is happening to my child, I want to know about it immediately. I wake up to you all over the news, and now you're splashed across the newspaper. I knew nothing good would come from that 'Sex Doctor' foolishness. If you had gone to medical school like your father, none of this would be happening. How am I going to explain this to my friends?"

Donathan blew out a heavy breath, drowning out his mother's words as she continued to ramble. Everything was always about status with Sylver Monet James. No matter where the conversation started, it always ended up there. He tried to remain calm, but that was the main reason he'd been avoiding calling her.

"Mom, why does everything always have to be about medical school?"

"Doctors lead nice, respectable lives, Donathan. They don't end up on the front page of the newspaper."

He groaned and spun around in his high-back leather chair. He pictured his mother perched behind her full-glass desk at her

Sotheby's real estate office. Flawlessly styled salt-and-pepper hair with an impeccably tailored St. John suit. He was sure she looked stunning, as she always did. But what rock had she crawled under? Austyn Greene was a doctor, and she led the headline.

"I would like to discuss this with you in person before your father's recognition celebration. When can you and Sydney come for dinner?"

"About Dad's party—I don't think this is a good time for me to be out in any public settings. The press is harassing me for a story, and I don't want to rain on Dad's parade—"

"That's pure nonsense. Your father would be utterly devastated if you missed his recognition dinner. He's worked so hard for this. And you shouldn't hide if you haven't done anything wrong. Besides, the dinner is not open to the public. We've bought out Pican's for a private invitation–only affair."

Donathan cringed. He didn't know if it was worse to be surrounded by strangers speculating and gawking at him, or his mother's bourgeois fake-ass friends.

"I'll check Sydney's schedule and get back to you."

"Boy, don't play with me. You have twenty-four hours to call me back, or I'll come to you."

CHAPTER 8

Clutching her Louis Vuitton tote bag, Sydney entered Children's Hospital a little apprehensive about what to expect from her colleagues. She had practically begged the hand surgeon to allow her to come back to work, but she didn't expect Human Resources to place her on the work schedule immediately, and after her run-in with Julia Stevens yesterday, she wasn't so sure if she was ready to do this after all.

What happened to her and Donathan was unthinkable—almost being killed by a madwoman. Austyn Greene had exhibited no mercy, and she was determined to harm them both. If Sydney had not alerted the authorities to their whereabouts before she entered the apartment they both would be dead. The knot in her gut loosened a bit. Helping children was what she'd been put on this earth to do, and she wasn't going to let gossip and whispers get in the way of that. She had done nothing wrong. She was the victim.

At this point, anything was better than being cooped up in the house with Donathan. The man drove her crazy, or maybe it was the guilt closing in on her. She wished she could rewind the situation back to that afternoon when she'd stumbled across the compromising photos of Donathan and Austyn Greene on the internet. Instead of packing her bags and taking up residence at the Waterfront Hotel, she should have stayed, talked to Donathan, not accused him and run away. It took him more than a week to come after her, but by the time she found out the truth about Austyn, it was too late. The invisible line that married women should steer clear of had already been crossed.

Naïvely, she moved back home, expecting her life to revert to the way she and Donathan were before Miles. In love, lounging in bed all day, or cooking and feeding one another, followed by the most exquisite lovemaking that made her toes curl. She longed for his demanding directives and the way he looked at her when she modeled the sexy lingerie and designer shoes he purchased for his very own private shows. Now he was obsessed with everything else except her. She didn't know where the old Donathan was, but she wanted him back.

Well, that wasn't exactly true. The paparazzi who were camped outside their front gates harassing them as they traveled about didn't help matters any, but ultimately it was her refusal to give him a definitive answer to whether she slept with Miles or not that had taken ahold of him and wouldn't let go. Every time he asked, she'd say things like, "I can't believe you keep asking me that," or "You need to quit obsessing about that and get it together." But that clearly wasn't good enough. Payton was actually right for once. Nothing good would come from him knowing that Miles Day had licked "his" kitty, except that she would lose her pedestal status permanently, and he would never look at her the same way ever again. But she couldn't keep this secret from him for the rest of their lives, could she? Sydney glanced at the palm of her hand. To the naked eye, the physical wound had healed, but the emotional scars needed more time.

Sydney took a seat at the nurses' station and logged into the intranet. After clocking in, she clicked on the tab labeled *Physicians' Schedules*. Then she scrolled down the names until she saw *Miles Day*. The schedules were listed for two months out, and according to the calendar, his shift would be ending now. Sydney sighed heavily. She didn't know why she even bothered checking. His name wasn't on the call board, and she was no closer to knowing where Miles was and when he was coming back. She contemplated calling Miles again. She just needed to hear his voice—to know if he was okay.

"Good morning, everyone," Dr. Julia Stevens said brightly. "Isn't it a lovely day?"

The nurses were in a shift meeting, so there was no "everyone" at the nurses' station . . . just Sydney. Sydney spun around to face the tall, thin woman with attractive features and expressive green eyes. She rolled her eyes upward as Julia tossed her shiny red hair over her shoulder.

"I can't believe you're here. You are such a brave soul. I mean, I would never be able to show my face around here again if my husband and lover got into a brawl and tore up the local breakfast spot."

"Excuse me?"

She leaned in close and whispered, "Oh, now, come on, Sydney. Everybody knew there was something going on with you two, and the mere fact that he's disappeared into thin air confirms my suspicions. You're the reason he's not here today."

"What do you mean, I'm the reason he's not here today?" Sydney asked, feeling her sense of confidence slip from her shoulders. "Since when did you become the expert on Miles?"

"For the record, Miles and I are quite chummy. As a matter of fact, I spoke with him yesterday."

"And said what?" Sydney asked, a little too defensively and now looking around to see if anyone could overhear their conversation.

"What we talked about is really none of your business, but he asked me to cover this shift for him. And I told him outright what a fool he was for getting involved with a married woman," Julia replied with a superior smirk. "And when we talk later tonight, I'm going to tell him that again."

Sydney stared at Julia in disbelief. There was not much love lost between the two women. She and Julia had always tolerated one another, but the redhead's cattiness and jealousy had gotten much worse since they'd all come back from the medical conference in Chicago.

"Look, Julia, I'm not sure how anything related to me, Miles, or my husband has become any of your business, but I'd appreciate it if you'd stop spreading rumors about things you know nothing about. And just in case I'm not being perfectly clear: What I'm saying to you is, mind your own damn business."

Sydney retreated toward the doctors' lounge, her mind firing questions. Where was Miles? Had he started a relationship with Julia? If that were true, she had no right to have feelings about it since, as Julia had pointed out, she was a married woman.

"Dr. James, is that you?" the head neonatal intensive care unit nurse called from the other end of the corridor. "I have a few babies who would love some of your tender love and care," she sang as she paused to enter a set of automatic double doors.

All Sydney wanted to do was get back to work and put this fiasco behind her, but Julia Stevens was determined to make her life a living hell. Maybe rocking a few babies would get her out of this funk.

"I'd love to cuddle with a few of your munchkins," Sydney called back to the woman. "Once the shift stabilizes, I'll be right down."

Sydney stepped into the doctors' lounge and studied her reflection in the mirror. She hated that evil jealous bitch. But right now she was the only connection to Miles, and if she kept Julia talking she would uncover all the information she needed to find out his whereabouts. Sydney blew out a ragged breath. She had to stop letting Julia ruffle her feathers like this.

CHAPTER 9

Austyn Greene turned off the television. How much longer could she stay holed up in this hellhole watching reruns of *The Maury Povich Show.* She couldn't believe how fucking gullible these people were. How many times did the asshole have to say, "You are not the father!" If a chick brought her man on the show to reveal a "secret," she'd cheated.

"Damn, it's not fucking rocket science," she hissed.

She couldn't watch another minute of this bullshit. A few nights ago, she'd left the motel and ended up at a place called Shaboom in San Ramon for a drastic, much-needed change in scenery. She needed to escape from this dump so she could think. She'd been extra careful and kept her head down, avoiding the eyes of everyone she saw as if people were taking a mental inventory of her face.

On the outside, she was sporting nude lips, a long blond wig that brushed the middle of her back, big earrings, a pair of green-colored contacts, skinny jeans, and form-fitting, revealing tops—a far cry from her usual designer attire.

However, on the inside, her mind was spinning in a hundred different directions, anxious to teach Donathan James a lesson about trying to stick his dick where it didn't belong. Yet what she longed for most was to witness the life seep out of Lois Greene's body. It was time for her to pay, and Lois was here in Pittsburg—she could feel it.

Austyn picked up the specimen jar off the bedside table and stared at the floating contents while fingering the scalpel in her pocket. Unfortunately, for him, during her little excursion to Shaboom's, the obnoxious prick just wouldn't leave her alone. He'd kept touching her and whispering all the disgusting things he wanted to do to her. He'd given her no choice except to make sure he wouldn't be bothering anyone else—ever. She shook the cylinder. These would do for now, but she wouldn't rest until she added Donathan's jewels to her collection.

Austyn made her way over to the closet, a nervous habit she'd developed, to check her duffel bag again. Money, drugs, and syringes—everything was right where she'd left them.

She picked up a stack of cash and found herself daydreaming about what her life would have been like if she had grown up with a normal mother and father—the two-parent American dream. But growing up in the Los Angeles foster care system, the repeated sexual abuse, multiple foster families, and group homes had been anything but normal. When she was fifteen, she decided she didn't want to end up like her mother, and with the help of a social worker, she learned the secret that most kids in the foster care system didn't take full advantage of. There were thousands of scholarships and other financial resources available to wards of the state.

When Austyn was thirteen, she was placed with a couple who were doctors for an emergency foster care placement. And even though she was whisked away at the end of thirty days, it was the safest she had ever felt in her life. That experience left a lasting impression on Austyn, so when the social worker asked what she wanted to study in college, she set her sights on becoming a doctor.

She clawed her way through undergraduate school, then stumbled into UCLA Medical School, and her hard work paid off. At twenty-five, she had the rest of her life to live. To shed all the bad things that happened to her. But then those bastards raped her, and her mind wouldn't shut up.

The voices in her head told her to do things, and it felt so good when she did. She stalked those bastards who violated her for weeks, and they had no idea she was even there. When the time was just right, she took their money, their drugs, and their lives, and she wouldn't rest until she did the same thing to Lois Greene.

The sudden shriek of a police siren startled her. Panicked, Austyn jumped up, placed the stack of cash back inside the duffel bag, and stuffed it into the hole she had cut in the closet floor. Was that the police? Were they here for her? She paced back and forth, retracing her steps from last night. After leaving that hotel in Pleasanton, she drove around for at least an hour before making her way back to Pittsburg. She was sure no one had followed her. Or had they? She couldn't go to jail. She had to finish what she came here to do.

You can't do nothing right, the voice spat inside her head. *I knew we couldn't trust you to pull this off.*

Austyn continued pacing, ignoring the conversation going on inside of her head. The voice spoke again.

The only thing you were supposed to do was make her pay for what you did to us. You're weak and pathetic.

"Shut the hell up!" Austyn yelled as the voices grew louder, and Austyn covered her ears with both hands to drown it all out. And then it came to her like a flash of light. The voices coming from the outside parking lot were that of a man and woman arguing. Why were the police arguing? She made her way over to the window so she could get a better view.

Holding her breath, Austyn peeped out the window and was surprised to see a man and a woman standing next to a midnight-blue Lexus. They weren't the cops as she'd first thought. The man was tall and lean, his cheeks sunk in due to his drug use. His eyes were glassy and he seemed irritable, but the woman was not from these parts. Austyn could only see the woman's profile, but every-thing about her was first class, from the expensive sunglasses that framed her flawless caramel face to the multiple gold bracelets that jangled loosely on her wrist. Austyn cracked open the window to better hear the exchange.

"Goddammit, Payton, give me my money. It wasn't your house, and it ain't your fucking money!" the crackhead said, his arms flailing around with noticeable sweat stains under both arms of his faded T-shirt.

"Uncle Sheldon, you need to calm down before they refuse to give you a room—"

"I don't give a damn! If you give me what's mine, we can end this shit right now!"

"I'm sorry, but I'm not giving you the money. I can't sit back and watch you smoke it all away. I'm putting your money into a trust account. We can find you a permanent place to live—"

"It's your damn fault I don't have a place to live in the first place."

"Maybe you're right, but erratic actions cause desperate measures. You gave me no choice. I couldn't allow you to trash the place like that. It's time for you to do something with your life."

"I am doing exactly what I want with MY life!"

"Look, here's the deal. We can search for a more suitable living arrangement and I'll give you a monthly allowance, but if you decide to go to rehab, upon completion of being clean for six months, then I will relinquish all control of your money over to you—"

"There you go with that rehab shit again. If you want me to go to rehab so bad, maybe I can see if they have an open bed next to yo mama!"

Austyn perked up. The woman removed her sunglasses, revealing a tightness across her face.

"Yeah, that's right. I said yo mama!" the man repeated with a smirk. "Lois Greene is right around the fucking corner, and if you want to mother somebody, maybe you should start with her."

Austyn stepped back from the window, her mind trying to make sense of what she had just heard. These people actually had ties to the bitch she was looking for. She quickly took a seat on the floor and situated her body closer to the curtains. She peeked out again.

The woman was quiet for what seemed like an eternity, as if evaluating how she should react. Not the kind like she was thinking, but the kind like she wanted to choke the shit out of him. Finally, she spoke.

"I'm beginning to think that this is a game to you," she said. "The last few times I've seen or talked to you, you snuck in a jab about that bitch. Did she put you up to this? Do you know where Lois Greene is?"

The man didn't respond. A haughty grin slowly spread across his bony face. "Wouldn't you like to know," he spat, mocking her. "Let's make a deal, niecy. If you give me my money, then I'll tell you where Lois is. Other than that, you can kiss my black ass," he said and stormed off with his bicycle in tow.

"I'll rent you the room for thirty days!" she screamed after him.

Austyn waited until the woman disappeared into the motel rental office before she hurried to the nightstand to grab a pad and pencil, then hurried back to the window to take down the license plate number of the dark-blue Lexus. She also scribbled down the names *Sheldon* and then *Payton*. Her luck couldn't get any better than this. Lois Greene was right around the corner. All she had to do was devise a plan for good ol' Uncle Sheldon to lead her right to her.

CHAPTER 10

"What the hell?" Donathan mumbled as he haphazardly pulled his car into the S-curved driveway. He cut the engine off and jumped out of the car. He had to stop her; heaven only knew what Barbara Brown was saying to those reporters.

"That crazy castration gal came by here numerous times, and I knew immediately that something wasn't right about her. Running 'round here slicing up folks like she ain't got the sense she was born with. That's the problem with these young folks today, somebody needs to take a strap to they behind—"

Before he could reach her, he was met by a barrage of random questions from the swarm of reporters.

"Dr. James, is it true the woman who held you hostage is wanted for questioning in the castration murders?"

"Were you two having an affair?"

"Is she going to have your baby?"

Donathan cringed, but stepped around the cluster of microphones, ignoring the questions.

"Mrs. Brown, may I speak with you for a moment?"

"Of course, sugah," the pecan-colored woman said with a reluctant smile. She made a few steps toward him, her multicolored housedress blowing in the wind. He placed his arms around her shoulders and escorted her the rest of the way across the street, away from the mob.

"Mrs. Brown, you have to really be careful with these people. Anything you say will be sensationalized and splashed across the front pages of the newspapers and on television, and that's the last thing I need right now."

"Well, you should have thought about that before you went gallivanting around town with that hussy. Herbert and I seen them pictures."

"Look, Mrs. Brown. I know it looks bad, but I'm innocent."

"Hmph," she said, folding her chubby arms across her bosom. "Ain't nothing worse than a wandering man."

"Didn't you just hear me say that I'm innocent?"

"Maybe if you quit talking that bedroom talk on the radio and dressing like you one of them fashion magazine models or something."

Donathan looked down at his black slacks and black dress shirt. He'd just finished a strategy meeting with the radio executives, finalizing how to incorporate him back on the air. Nothing "fashion magazine" about it.

"Mrs. Brown, I'm serious. I didn't do anything wrong."

"I heard you, but actions speak louder than words, and innocent men don't hide from the truth. They speak it. I been living here twenty years, and have never seen the likes of this foolishness," she said, gesturing to the pack across the street. "They remind me of a flock of chickens waiting to be tossed some feed."

"Exactly! They just want anything they can use to continue to defame my name."

"Your name?" She perched both hands on her wide hips. "What about Sydney's name? Maybe if you just give them something, it will tide them over for a bit."

It was Donathan's turn to survey the pack. He had been so wrapped up in his own issues he hadn't stopped to think about how this was affecting Sydney. He would begin his amends with dinner in the city tonight. But first, a quick drive over the bridge to pick up a little pink box from Agent Provocateur and a new pair of stilettos would put a smile on her face and his. And maybe Mrs. Brown was right. It did seem like the more he ignored them, the more they hounded him for a story. And he was tired of the constant media escorts. At this point, he didn't care what it took. He just wanted his life back. He turned back to Barbara Brown, who had already begun making her way up the stairs leading to her front door.

"Mrs. Brown, if you see any sign of Austyn Greene, call the police immediately," he called after her.

When Barbara Brown reached the top of the stairs, she turned and waved to her paparazzi friends behind him.

"Don't you worry, son. I got the police on speed dial, but with all these budget cuts, let's just hope they show up."

Donathan pivoted and walked toward the pack, his strides long and confident.

"Alright. I'm going to answer a few questions for you guys, then you're to stop camping out in front of my house and office? Is that a deal?"

"Have you heard from Austyn Greene?"

"No."

"Has there been any sign of her?"

"No."

"Why did she try to kill you?"

Relieved that the questions weren't as provocative as he imagined they would be, Donathan shrugged his shoulders.

"No one knows the answer to that except Austyn Greene, and once the detectives locate her, I hope we will all find that out."

He took a few more questions, and just like that the reporters were gone. When Donathan got into his car, instead of continuing through the security gates, he backed up, watched the gates close, and headed back down Moeser Lane toward the freeway. He had more than enough time to pick up those items for Sydney and get a nap in before their date tonight.

Donathan parked his Mercedes next to the curb outside the Hillstone Restaurant, off the Embarcadero. He exited the car and hurried around to the passenger side to open the door for his wife. Sydney took the hand he offered and didn't let go once her Jimmy Choos hit the pavement.

He pulled her into him and kissed her lips lightly, inhaling her scents of lavender and coconut oil before his silent gaze captured hers again. He smiled, still holding her by the hand, and headed toward the cozy brick building. Once they reached the door, he held it open, admiring the chocolate-brown slip dress that brushed across her sexy lean frame in all the right places.

"Reservation for James," he said.

"Right this way."

The hostess gathered two menus and escorted the couple to a coveted booth next to the fireplace. The place was practically deserted for late summer, but evenings in San Francisco reached temperatures in the mid to low fifties, cool and breezy at night, making this the perfect place for sitting next to a burning flame.

After the server left with their food orders, Donathan scooted in closer.

"I can't wait to taste you," he whispered in Sydney's ear, feeling a familiar tightening in his groin.

"Maybe we should have stayed home," she murmured, turned on by his baritone bass vibrating in her ear.

Donathan eased his hand underneath the table and parted Sydney's legs.

"What are you doing?" she whispered.

"What do you think?"

For a moment, Donathan caressed her bare thighs before his fingertips wandered higher and seized her lace thong.

"Relax, baby," he persuaded. "Nobody is paying any attention to us." He pushed her panties to the side and stroked her center. Sydney's eyes glistened with arousal. She quickly surveyed the room, then did as he asked, her body melting into the high-back booth. Donathan touched her in the way he knew she liked to be touched. The more he massaged, the wetter she got. Next, he inserted one, then two fingers and watched her hips roll forward, chasing the pressure he was putting on her G-spot.

"You like that?" he whispered in her ear.

"Uhm-hmm," she purred.

The beauty of her contorted face and swallowed moans made him want to put her up on the table and make love to her right there. She was so fucking sexy. Suddenly, her walls contracted around his fingers, and he knew he'd hit the jackpot. He was so caught up in his own visual foreplay that it took him a few seconds to realize that his cell phone was vibrating in his jacket pocket.

He reluctantly removed his hand from underneath her slip dress and licked his fingers as he examined the screen of his iPhone with his free hand. It was Holsey, the private investigator, a number he'd memorized.

"I need to take this." He scooted out of the booth, adjusted his black slacks, and pulled down his black zip-front cashmere pullover to conceal his erection. Once out of earshot, he swiped across the screen and accepted the call.

"This is Donathan."

"Curtis Holsey, here," he said, his voice hoarse and scratchy like sandpaper. "There's been another murder."

"Fuck! Where? How do you know it's her?"

"Not a lot of serial killers going around castrating their victims. They found the guy at a motel in Pleasanton."

"Are you close to finding her?"

"You're not paying me to find her. Our deal is to find the mother. This tidbit of information is just because I thought you should know. They found the victim last night. The cops are trying to keep a lid on it."

"So, what do we do now?"

"I'll continue to do what you're paying me to do. In the meantime, I'd suggest you watch your back."

★ ★ ★

Donathan ended the call and took a deep, cleansing breath, then walked back toward the table. By the time he got there, his disposition had visibly changed.

"What's wrong?"

"That was the private detective I hired to locate Austyn Greene."

Sydney stiffened. "I thought the police were handling that?"

He eased into the booth, but this time he kept his distance. "It's been three weeks, and they don't seem any closer to finding her."

"I still think you should let the professionals handle it."

Donathan let out a bark of laughter. "Those *professionals* didn't see fit to contact me about a dead body they found in a hotel room in Pleasanton last night. The MO has Austyn Greene written all over it."

Horror washed over Sydney's face. "What?"

"Exactly," he said knowingly. "I got caught sleeping the last time, but I'm not about to be blindsided by them—or you, for that matter—again."

Sydney glared at him, somewhat perplexed before she responded. "What's that supposed to mean?"

"I've asked you outright about your relationship with Miles Day."

"'Relationship'?" she said, her anger welling up in her eyes. "Miles and I are colleagues, but I should be the one asking questions about your 'relationship'," she said, using her fingers to show air quotes, "with Austyn Greene. Like how the hell did you end up in her hotel room anyway?"

This time his eyes sliced into her. He had been married to this woman for the past eight years. He knew her well, and she was hiding something.

"This is not about me, and don't give me that 'colleague' bullshit!"

"Will you lower your voice? I've had enough of being embarrassed by you," she hissed.

Checking his anger, he leaned back and exhaled. He couldn't

think straight. He hadn't meant for this to happen. He'd planned the evening like old times, including the new lingerie and Louboutins he'd left for her on her side of the bed. He didn't want the evening to end like this.

"I feel like we can't have a normal conversation anymore. Why do we keep digressing to this?"

He saw pain etched on her face. He looked down at his knuckles, the scarring barely visible, then back up to Sydney.

"Because something happened between you and Miles, and since you refuse to be honest with me about it, I'm going to ask him, man to man, myself."

CHAPTER 11

After an hour of bumper-to-bumper traffic jams and stuntman maneuvers, Tony eased his black Ford Escalade into his narrow driveway.

He checked his watch: It was almost seven in the evening, much earlier than the usual time he arrived home. For the past few years, unbeknownst to anyone, Tony took classes at night to finish up his bachelor's degree at Cal State East Bay, and he was one final away from realizing his dream. Not only did he want to make his mother proud by becoming the first person in his family to obtain any type of degree, but he also had his sights set on transitioning to a management position. He wasn't getting any younger, and he wanted more. More for himself and now more for his sister.

Today was his first day back at work since his mother's passing, and getting on and off the UPS truck had taken a serious toll on him. His body ached everywhere. All he wanted to do right now was jump in a hot shower and hit the sack hard, but first, he had to figure out what to do with his sister.

"Tony!" Najee squealed, stepping off the porch stroking the calico kitten he'd given to her in the wake of their mother's death.

At fifteen, Najee Barnes looked a lot like pictures of Shirley Barnes, their mother, at the same age: tall and slender with a head full of wavy brown hair that rested in ringlets just past her shoulders. She'd developed into a beautiful girl with a fierce streak of independence. She wore flip-flops, hip-hugging jeans flared just right, and layers of multicolored tank tops—typical attire for a sixteen-year-old.

As soon as he opened the car door, she threw herself into him, wrapping her free arm around his body, hugging him tight. Two teenage boys riding bicycles called out to her. "What's up, Najee?" They both grinned and waved.

"Well, hello to you, too, beautiful." He kissed her on the forehead and held on to her a little longer. His eyes tracked the young men as they pedaled past. He'd lived here for several years and couldn't remember the last time he'd seen boys on bicycles riding past his house. And since Najee attended school in Berkeley, they couldn't be her classmates.

"How do you know those guys?" he asked with suspicion.

"Oh, that's just Tim and Jayden."

"Do they live around here?"

"Yeah, around the corner. I met them when Aunt Rosemary and I took a walk one day."

Why was this the first time he'd heard anything about her meeting boys who lived around the corner? He was definitely going to have a talk with his aunt about this. He thought back to what it was like being sixteen, and the last thing he needed was some slick-ass boys sniffing around. That wasn't going to happen on his watch. As far as he was concerned, Najee Simone Barnes would not be dating until she graduated college and was at least twenty-five.

Arm in arm, they made their way toward the three-bedroom bungalow framed by freshly cut grass and neatly trimmed bushes. He took pride in his home just like his neighbors did.

"Why were you sitting out here?" he said, looking around for nothing in particular. For a bachelor, his neighborhood was pretty safe, but for a sixteen-year-old girl, he was beginning to think that maybe he wasn't so sure.

"I was waiting for you. Can I go to the movies with Lauren and Nicole?"

"Naj, I don't think that's a good idea. I'm exhausted, and it's a weeknight—"

"C'mon, Tony, pleeeaaasssse," she whined, letting the kitten down. "It's summertime, and I'll be back home by ten. Maybe you can go out on a date with Payton. She left two messages for you today. Who is she anyway?"

"Nobody you need to worry about."

"Pleeeeeaaassse," she begged as if her life depended on it.

He stared down at her. Over the past few months, she'd been through a lot. Moving to the Oakland/San Leandro border from Berkeley had to be a huge culture shock for her. She was the true epitome of an independent urban kid. She could get to anywhere in the Bay Area she needed to go on the bus or the BART. He couldn't even do that himself. Hell, it wasn't too long ago that he had ridden the BART to Bay Point for the first time when he'd met up with Payton to help her evict Sonya Mitchell.

Najee held his gaze. Finally, he looked away to deflect her big brown eyes before they turned him into putty. He was tired and didn't feel like going back out. All he wanted to do was take a hot shower and hit the sack. Besides, teenagers didn't go to the movies on weeknights, or did they? It just wasn't safe for her to be wandering around at night. He blew out a ragged breath.

"Sorry, kid, but I'm going to have to say no. How about you go to the movies this weekend? I can drop you off and pick you up."

"Drop me off? Are you cray?" she said, using teenage slang for "crazy." "I'm not a five-year-old. I don't need you to drop me off. I have friends who drive, or I can catch the bus. I did some research, and I know what buses I need to catch."

Drive? Now, that was another thing. He didn't like the idea of her riding in cars with a bunch of newly licensed teenagers. He was going to have to teach her to drive, and then use some of the insurance money he'd entrusted for her to purchase a car of her own. He shuddered at that thought, too. How the hell did parents raise kids without stressing themselves to death?

"Well?" Najee asked, a determined look in her eyes. "Are you going to let me go or not?"

"Look, Naj, the thing is, it's just not safe for a young girl to be traipsing around town after dark. There's a lot going on in Oakland—"

"If Mom were alive, she'd let me go," she said, her brown eyes filling with tears.

"Well, I'm not Mom," he snapped, "and my answer is no."

A barrage of tears began rolling down her cheeks. "You never let me go anywhere," she yelled, the tears flowing faster.

Shit. He reached for her and pulled her tightly into his embrace. "I know this is hard for you, Naj, but it's hard for me, too."

"You can't keep me cooped up in this house."

He dried her tears with the pads of his thumbs and tilted her face up to him. "I was talking to Donathan, and he's going to talk with Sydney about hanging out with you a few days a week. What do you think about that?"

"I'm not a kid. I don't need a babysitter."

"I know you're not a kid, but I think it would be nice for you to, you know, hang out with a girl."

She twisted her face at his comment. "My friends are girls."

"Najee, c'mon. You know exactly what I mean." He looked on helplessly as the tears started again.

"This is not fair!" She stormed off to her room and slammed the door behind her.

Tony was silent for a moment. He stood there replaying what had just happened. His aunt had warned him that sometimes as a parent he would have to make tough, unfavorable decisions, but he hadn't expected a movie to be the cause of their first real standoff. If this was any indication of what was to come, he couldn't imagine what the exchange was going to look like when they had their talk about boys. He sighed heavily. He had his hands full.

CHAPTER 12

Payton hurried around the smooth dark waters of Lake Merritt, contemplating her next move. She had not heard from Sheldon in a few days. And with his track record, she knew by now he'd blown through the money she gave him. Did he think his silence would convince her to turn over his inheritance money? Well, if he did, he had another think coming. With every step she took, she racked her brain, trying to figure out just what her uncle was up to. How dare he threaten her with anything related to Lois Greene? He should have known that if he wanted anything from her, then using Lois Greene as leverage was to his disadvantage. She couldn't shake the feeling that something more was going on. Was he trying to scam her? Or was he out scamming somebody else to get his high? The thought of this scared her more than giving him his money. If he was scamming people, sooner or later, it would all catch up to him, and she prayed nobody would hurt him.

He was a shell of the man she once remembered, and it saddened her to think about his demise. But that's exactly what would happen if she stood by and watched him smoke all he had left in this world in a crack pipe. She had to convince him that she was trying to help his dumb ass; well, maybe "dumb" wasn't the right word, considering his latest shenanigans.

"Fuck!" she yelled, dodging piles of geese droppings that covered the sidewalk and the mob of geese fighting for pieces of bread a mother and her young child were tossing to them from a bench. She rolled her eyes upward at the sign that explained why these nasty animals weren't dead. Killing them would be a federal offense, and nobody wanted to end up in jail for killing a damn bird. They were noisy, nasty, and very territorial about their babies, which was something all parents were supposed to be. Unfortunately for her, Lois Greene hadn't gotten the memo.

Her daddy, Jimmy, was the love of her life. The first day of school, the day she lost her first tooth, trips to the park, dyeing Easter eggs, and even painting her toenails, were all memories of her father. He took care of her. After he was murdered, everything changed. First, Lois demanded that Payton stop calling her "Mommy," claiming it made people think she was old. Gradually Lois started locking herself in her room, then hanging out with strange people, which eventually led to her leaving for days at a time with no explanation. Payton remembered living in a constant state of fear that she would wake up and her mother would be gone. And one day that fear came true.

Twenty-five years had passed, but Payton could still feel the devastation. It felt like it was yesterday that Lois left her standing outside the movie theater and never came back for her. After a few hours had passed, theater security contacted her grandparents, who were there in a matter of minutes to pick her up. Deep inside, she would always be the little girl who wasn't good enough for her mother to love. Lois didn't want her then, and Payton damn sure didn't want Lois now. So, what was it? Why would Lois come back here after all this time? She wanted something, and the logical explanation was money. Payton chuckled.

"I'll burn in hell before I give that bitch one dime," she said out loud.

In hindsight Lois abandoning her was probably one of the best fucking things she could have ever done for her. The fact that Lois Greene was rotting in rehab says her life turned out to be a fucking disaster, which is just what she deserved. And Payton was grateful that she wasn't a part of it. This abandoned little girl had made it. She was college-educated, with her own money and living life on her terms. Not too shabby for a girl with a crackhead mama.

When she rounded the lake, a brown UPS truck at the stoplight caught her attention. It had been weeks since she saw him standing outside the window at Pican's, and she still hadn't heard back from Tony. She'd texted and called him, but short of showing up on his doorstep unannounced, there was nothing else she could or would do. Effective immediately, she was done kissing his ass. If he didn't want to call her back, then fuck him. His loss. The string of lights hugging the perimeter of the lake flickered on, and Payton stared across the still water. She could see the Lake Chalet nestled in the distance and the multicolored rowboats neatly lined outside the sailboat house before locating her apartment building.

She counted the windows across the ninth floor of One Lakeside Drive, until she came to her own, and found herself reminiscing about the last time Tony had pressed her naked body into the cool floor-to-ceiling glass and fucked her senseless. She shuddered at the thought. He wasn't a selfish lover. He always took his time and worshiped every inch of her, including her mind. Tony Barnes always knew exactly what to do to get her off. Hell, who was she kidding? He was exactly what she craved right now, and those thoughts scared her so badly her stomach cramped.

She had broken her cardinal rule, which was to not let herself get emotionally involved with men. Physically, yes, she enjoyed a good time, but she had always made it clear from the beginning that a relationship was out of the question. She was always in control, and when the fun was over, she walked away. Not the other way around.

After finishing the three-mile loop, Payton made it back to her condo and found David Bryant sitting in the lobby.

"Hey," Payton said as he stood to greet her.

David was a coffee-with-a-splash-of-cream-colored man, immaculately dressed in a suit and tie. Although he was fifty-five years old, other than his slightly graying temples, he didn't look a day over forty. He grinned, flashing a perfect set of white teeth and a mischievous smile. He lowered his sunglasses—an accessory he no longer needed because it was getting dark out.

"So, are we going out or what?" he asked, scrutinizing her up and down, but lingering on her breasts.

Payton hesitated. She'd agreed to see him tonight, but now all she wanted to do was take a hot shower and lie on her chaise lounge for the rest of the evening, catching up on recorded episodes of *Power*.

"I guess," she said, turning on her heels to head for the elevators.

"Well, don't sound so excited about it. If you want, we can always order in," he said, trailing behind her.

They stepped into the elevator on opposite sides, and the doors closed behind them.

"So, where's wifey tonight?" Payton asked as the elevator ascended.

David shot her a sharp look. "Does it matter?"

Payton shrugged, feigning innocence. "I merely asked a simple question."

"If you must know, she's out of town," he said flatly.

"Her little trips sure have become more frequent over the past few months. I know Sharon's a high-profile entertainment attorney, but if I were you, I'd pay a little closer attention to that. Well, that's if you give a damn—"

"Are we staying in or going out?" he said, cutting her off, his words laced with agitation.

When Payton reached her front door, she punched in the code and turned back around to face him. His eyes were dark and brooding. She studied his expression a moment, imagining his after-five shadow prickling against the inside of her thighs. If they stayed in, she wouldn't have to get dressed. She could take a hot shower, fuck her way to multiple orgasms, and then she'd send his ass home, just like she always did. She grabbed him by his loosened tie and backed her way into the marble foyer.

"C'mon, take a shower with me and we can order in. What do you feel like eating?"

"The same thing I always eat when you and I are together," David said, using his foot to close the door behind them.

"And what's that?"

"You."

CHAPTER 13

It was almost noon when Sydney dragged herself out of bed. Last night, after she'd argued with Donathan at the restaurant, they drove home in complete silence. How dare he take out his frustrations on her? When they arrived home, she hurried up the stairs and slammed and locked the bedroom door behind her to send him a clear message. His ass was not sleeping with her tonight. But when she turned on the lights and saw the black shoebox and Agent Provocateur bag resting on her side of the bed, she almost gave in.

The guilt mixed with anger and humiliation kept her awake until the wee hours of the morning. She tossed and turned, tried not to inhale his overpowering scent that lingered on the pillows. The rift between them seemed so big, and she had no idea how to fix it. For the first time, she was afraid. Scared that what she and Donathan had gone through might be too much to overcome.

She made her way to the bathroom and stared at her reflection in the wall-to-wall mirror that stretched the length of the his and hers vanity.

"Oh, God," she groaned.

Her eyes were red and puffy, and her usually flat-ironed hair was a tangled mess, but with her hand still healing, there was not much she could do but wash it and be grateful for the natural curls she'd inherited from her mother.

★ ★ ★

After a quick shower, Sydney made her way downstairs. She could hear the soul-stirring sounds of Robert Glasper coming from the home office. When she reached the office doorway, she stretched her arms above her head, then leaned into the doorjamb surveying the scene. Donathan's clothes from last night were tossed across a chair and a throw blanket was bunched up on the couch. From the looks of things, he had not gotten much sleep last night either.

"I don't want to fight with you anymore," she said softly.

Donathan looked up from the folder he was reading and studied her. His gaze was so intense she had to look away.

"Come here."

When she reached him, she lifted her bare leg across his lap and straddled him. Immediately, the pads of his thumbs brushed against her beaded nipples, pressing hard against the jersey fabric. Then he rested his head on her chest listening to her heartbeat.

After a few minutes of making out, they came up for air. Sydney glanced over her shoulder at the cluttered desktop. It was covered with his usual black file folders, but the blue one resting open on top was the one she was most concerned about. She repositioned her body so she was now facing the desk.

"Did you get any sleep last night?"

He rested his forehead on her back and shook his head from side to side. "No."

"When was the last time you slept?"

"Yesterday, and before you ask, I didn't take a sleeping pill because I'm not interested in anything mind-altering right now."

Sydney's heart broke for him. From a medical perspective, she understood her husband had been traumatized, and truth be told, so had she. But his obsession with Austyn Greene was not healthy.

"Baby, you can't keep functioning on no sleep." She picked up Austyn Greene's dossier. "This can't continue."

Sydney was sure Donathan had gone over this file backward and forward numerous times and no new epiphanies were going to jump off those pages. He needed to let it go.

"I have to catch up on these patient files—"

"No, you don't. You're not seeing patients right now, remember? What you're doing is obsessing when what you need to do is leave the detective work to the police. I'm sure they'll find her soon."

"No, they won't."

"They're better equipped to find her than you are." She closed the blue file on the desk in front of him.

Between his unpredictable behavior, the tension between them, and their fighting, she just wanted her husband back. She turned back to face him.

"You can't keep doing this."

She watched him closely. She could almost see his inability to process; it was like he was trying to decipher what she was saying to him. Clearly, he was tired.

"Come lie down with me." She stood and reached for his hand. Before he could rise to his feet, she noticed a cream-colored envelope with lavender script addressed to Donathan James and Dr. Sydney James. She picked it up.

"What's this?" she asked, not waiting for his response as she removed the contents from the envelope. Her eyes skimmed the words:

Mrs. Sylver Monet James
invites you to a dinner honoring
Dr. Maurice James, the recipient of the prestigious
Dodson Medical Society Award
Saturday, May 15th @ 7:00 p.m.
Pican's
Black Tie Attire (invitation only)

"Oh my God!" Sydney squealed, practically jumping up and down. "This is fantastic! I can't believe your mother hasn't called."

Instantly, her mind raced back to the call she'd ignored from Sylver James. Yesterday, she let a call from her mother-in-law go to voice mail, sure that she was calling to voice her disapproval of Donathan being splashed across the front page of the Bay Area newspapers, but she was probably calling about this. Then again, knowing her mother-in-law, Sydney probably had it right the first time.

Donathan rolled his eyes upward. "My mother has done nothing but call me. I told her that we should probably sit this thing out—"

"What?"

"The last thing I want to do is ruin this night for my father."

"Donathan, you can't be serious." Her father-in-law worked hard and deserved the recognition. But at the same time, she understood Donathan's resistance, which had nothing to do with Austyn Greene. Raised with a silver spoon practically shoved down his throat, he was always reluctant when it came to mingling with the Bay Area elite. But not attending his father's recognition dinner wasn't an option.

"This will be a really big night for your father. He'll be devastated if you aren't there."

Donathan leaned back in the black leather chair and blew out a ragged breath. Sydney looked on in silence while he mulled over his options.

"Okay," he said, finally.

She rewarded his decision with a light kiss that turned into something of the more passionate variety before she finally pulled away and started for the door. Donathan gently tugged at her wrist.

"Wait, where are you going?"

"To check to see if your tux needs to be cleaned."

"Slow down, baby. We have almost a week. Besides, I thought we were going to lie down," he said, motioning toward the stiff appendage bulging in his pajama bottoms. His stomach growled.

Lounging around in bed with her man was high on her list of favorite things to do. But first, she needed to cook him something to eat.

"Do you want some grits and eggs? I can whip up a quick omelet."

Donathan lifted her right hand. The white gauze wraps were gone, but a flesh-colored two-by-four bandage covered her entire palm.

"Maybe I should do the cooking," he said.

"I got this. I can't do surgery yet, but I am allowed to cook up some grits and a few eggs."

CHAPTER 14

"You're up early," Austyn said, eyeballing the tall, lanky man anxiously wandering around the motel parking lot. The man's clothing draped over his body like the extra skin of a Japanese Shar-Pei. His dark brown eyes were wide and wired, his hair a tangled mess of dreads. Her target was primed and ready.

"You need something to take the edge off?" Austyn questioned, thinking this was the exact moment she had been waiting for over the last few days.

"What?" Sheldon mumbled. "Girl, quit playin' with me and stick to what you do best, which is make your money lying on your back. Now, move out my way," he said, attempting to step around her.

Austyn fished inside her jacket pocket and pulled out a small plastic baggie with yellowish rocklike contents. Sheldon quickly reached for the bag, but she yanked it away.

"Not so fast."

"Bitch, gimme my shit!" he yelled.

Several motel room doors flew open, the occupants peeking out to see what all the commotion was. Austyn stuffed the coveted contents back into her pocket and backed out of his reach.

"Who you callin' a bitch? And last time I checked, this wasn't your shit!"

"C'mon, girl, stop playing," he begged, closing the distance she'd put between them.

Austyn felt around in her other pocket for her scalpel, before she made the next proposition. Because even in his cracked-out state, Sheldon was still a man and he still outweighed her. She noticed Ray, the motel pimp, watching them closely, and she didn't need the likes of him all up in her business. She needed to take these negotiations behind closed doors.

"You can have this," she said, patting her pocket, "but first, I need you to answer a few questions for me."

"What do you want?" he said, his voice laced with desperation.

"C'mon, let's go to your room."

Sheldon practically ran across the parking lot with Austyn close on his heels. His hands shook as he inserted the key into the door to gain entry into his room. Once inside, he pleaded, "Give it to me. I'll tell you anything you want to know."

Austyn extended her hand, and he grabbed the tiny clear bag and rushed into the bathroom, closing and locking the door behind him. A few minutes passed before the strange odor wafted from underneath the door. The burning plastic smell transported her back to her childhood—the little girl being dragged in and out of crack houses.

In medical school, she'd learned that it wasn't the cocaine that smelled when it was smoked; it was the chemicals used to cut it. Holding her breath, she coughed, then placed her ear to the bathroom door, listening for any indication of what was going on in there. Silence.

"Sheldon," she called out, hoping she hadn't given him too much. Austyn jiggled the handle of the locked door. The last thing she needed was for him to overdose and her not get the information she needed. The cops would be swarming around here for sure. Working herself into a panic, she called out his name again.

"Sheldon!"

Too many people had seen her come in here, and if he was dead, she would be the first person they came looking for. Making sure she didn't touch anything, she started to back away from the bathroom door, then she heard his weak response.

"What?" he mumbled.

"You ready to talk?"

"Damn, can I at least enjoy my high for a few minutes?" he said, slurring like his mouth was full of marbles. "We can talk tomorrow," he shot back.

Austyn was prepared for this move, but she second-guessed whether she should give him the second bag of crack. The first one was the bait, but she needed the second one to catch the big fish. The sooner she got the information she needed, the less likely she would be involved in an overdose.

"There's more where that came from," she said, her voice trailing off. She stood her ground and waited. And it wasn't long before the bathroom door flew open and a pair of glassy eyes stared back at her. His cheeks looked sucked in, and his dark brown skin looked ashen.

"Tell me about the woman you were with the other day."

"What woman?"

"The one driving the Lexus?"

"Why you asking 'bout her?"

"I'm the one asking the questions, not you," Austyn snapped. She removed the motivation from her pocket so he could see it.

"Her name is Payton, she's my niece, and the uppity little bitch won't give me my goddamn money," he said, his words venomous and thick.

"What money?"

"My inheritance. You sure got a lot of questions." He pushed past her and made his way toward the bed.

This slow-moving creature was a stark contrast to the man who walked around the grounds like he owned the damn place.

Now she could barely get him to string more than two words together at a time. Her plan to let him take a hit, then try to have a conversation had been a bad one. He took a seat on the floor and nestled his back into the corner. The room didn't have much light, but she could see the beads of sweat forming on his forehead.

"Why won't she give you your money?"

"Because she knows I'm going to smoke it up," he said matter-of-factly.

"Does your sister, Lois Greene, have an inheritance, too?"

Sheldon frowned. "How da fuck do you know Lois? She hasn't lived around here for years."

Austyn flicked the baggie again and shook her head.

"I ain't got no sisters. She's my sister-in-law."

Austyn's mind connected the genealogy dots. If Lois Greene was Sheldon's sister-in-law, then he wasn't related to her by blood. But she'd overheard him referring to Lois Greene as Payton's mother. If that were the case, then she and Payton were half sisters.

"So, how is Lois related to your niece, Payton?"

"You ain't the sharpest knife in the drawer. She's her got-damn mama," he said, clearly sounding frustrated. "How much longer we gon' play twenty questions?"

Now, it was time for the real questions that would lead her to the reason she came to Pittsburg in the first place. But it really didn't matter whether Sheldon helped her or if she had to comb every inch of this town to find Lois Greene her damn self. One way or another, she would get exactly what she came to Pittsburg for.

"Last question," she said before placing the plastic baggie on the small circular table. The hunger in his eyes rose to the surface.

"Where is Lois Greene?"

"The judge sent her to Glover House, the drug treatment facility," he blurted out. He stood to his feet, his agitation clearly visible.

"I need to see her."

"She can't have visitors for at least two weeks—"

"Do you know where Glover House is?"

"No, but I can find out."

Austyn picked up his cell phone and began typing. "Tell you what, I'm going to save my number in your phone, and when you get me an address for Glover House, I've got plenty more of this just for you." She reached into her jacket pocket, tossed an extra baggie on the table, and backed out of the room, closing the door behind her. She hoped he didn't do anything stupid, like have a heart attack or a stroke. She kind of liked the arrogant bastard. But crack was such a nasty drug. It made people sell their souls and their children, chasing a high that would never be as good as the first time they took a hit. It was ironic that the same white crumbs that had devastated her life were now leading her down a trail right back to her mother.

Back in her room, Austyn chained the door and removed the laptop from her backpack. It booted up quickly, and after she typed in *Glover House, Pittsburg, CA,* she waited as the screen populated with several different links.

Austyn grinned and clicked on the first hyperlink, and within seconds the website populated the laptop screen. She clicked, then clicked again, searching each page for the physical location of the facility, but came up empty. Every link she searched listed the address as a post office box.

"Fuck!" she hissed.

It looked like she was going to be depending on the crackhead more than she thought, but she had plenty of little baggies to keep him doing whatever she needed him to do.

CHAPTER 15

Donathan parked the car alongside the curb outside the posh eatery. He made it a point to keep his finger on the pulse of the new and happening spots in the Bay Area, yet somehow he'd never heard of this restaurant before. The outward façade reeked of his mother. Exclusive and private, two things Sylver James and her upscale clientele required. His mother was known for patronizing elite establishments, and before stepping a foot inside Donathan already knew this place fit the bill.

It had been two days since Sylver had threatened him in her own way, and before she showed up on his doorstep and encountered the paparazzi, he'd instructed his receptionist to phone her back immediately and set up a face-to-face meeting at a location of her choosing.

He sat in the car a moment to gather his thoughts. There was no explanation for his behavior, and playing the victim with his mother was not going to work. In all honesty, he had crossed the line the moment he decided to walk Austyn Greene to her hotel room—a tiny detail he'd expected to be magnified by Sydney long before now. But she hadn't pressed him on this significant issue, a fact that concerned him. With Sylver James, he wouldn't be so lucky.

There was a closed sign on the front window, but the brown

wooden door opened and Donathan was greeted by a young man who welcomed him inside, then escorted him through the establishment to a door marked private before walking away. Donathan mentally prepared himself for the barrage of questions that were coming, then stepped inside.

Before he could take a seat, Sylver was on her feet, demanding to know what the hell was going on.

"I cannot believe you have disrespected yourself in this manner, let alone me and your father. Did you know that your face has been splashed across every gossip rag in this country? God knows I taught you better than this. That woman has whore flashing like a neon sign across her forehead and for the life of me I can't wrap my brain around why my son would be caught dead with such trash," she said, shaking her head and flinging her hand in the air as if banishing the idea.

Donathan stared at the petite woman in front of him, the epitome of perfection. Her hair was coiffed just right, her dress was custom fit, she had the perfect shoes, and her accessories included the coveted Birkin handbag, a symbol that spoke volumes about his mother whenever she stepped into any room. Sylver turned on her heel, returned to her seat, and waited with a look of disdain on her face for Donathan to take his seat and join her.

Confrontations with his mother always conjured up feelings of failure, and today was no exception. He could see her disappointment and feelings of sorrow rising closer to the surface with every word. He had broken the cardinal rule by bringing palpable shame to the James name, and no matter what he did or said to justify his behavior, the reasoning would never be enough in the eyes of Sylver James.

His mother thrived on being the talk of the town for good reasons such as having a home in the right zip code, sending him to the appropriate schools, and being the wife of a prestigious doctor. But never for the bad or the ugly, something she'd instilled in him from day one. The truth was, he knew his mother loved him, but she didn't love the fact that he chose a life different from the one she'd envisioned for him. Holding his mother's gaze, Donathan took a seat.

"Are you done?"

"Don't you sass me, boy."

He reached for his mother's hand and kissed it lightly, then gave her a thousand-watt smile.

"You look absolutely stunning today, Sylver."

"Donathan Maurice James! How many times have I told you not to call me by my first name?" she said, unable to hide a slight grin. He winked at her and she quickly looked away. "Flattery will get you nowhere."

"Mom, look. You know I would never do anything to bring this type of attention to you and Dad. This entire thing has taken on a life of its own, but I handled it—"

"Are you referencing the statement you gave to the local channels the other day that they're playing on a loop along with the one from that dreadful woman who lives across the street from you? She is the exact reason I begged you and Sydney not to purchase property in El Cerrito. If you lived in a gated community none—"

"Mom, our home is behind a gate."

"You know exactly what I mean. If you lived in a respectable community those cameras wouldn't be able to come anywhere near your home. And what does Sydney think about all of this? I'm surprised the girl hasn't gone running scared..." his mother said, her voice trailing off.

Donathan sighed heavily, ruminating on her last words. When things got uncomfortable his wife did have a propensity to run, and the last time she had run straight into the arms of another man.

"You need help framing your story and creating a clear message for your brand. Is that torrid radio show you work for helping with damage control? Well, obviously not. You need a PR professional," she said, reaching for her purse, which had a personal seat at the table. "I have a referral for—"

"Mom, who cares what people think? I'm not one of your

clients," he snapped, growing agitated by the truths Sylver spoke. He didn't want to admit that everything his mother said was true. He hated the fact that the conversation had been commandeered by the reality of outward appearances—something he'd grown to despise—but he couldn't keep running from the inevitable.

"First of all, you need to watch your tone. Second, I know exactly who you are," she spat back. "I went through forty-eight hours of labor before giving birth to you. You are my child and I can see that you're hurting. So why on earth would you not think that I only want what's best for you?"

Donathan looked away. Everything his mother was saying was spot on. He was a local celebrity "brand" and between the things that happened with Austyn Greene and that damn altercation at Lois the Pie Queen his "brand" did need a little resuscitation.

"Well, at least we both agree on the fact that my brand has some serious issues right now and this is the exact reason why I told Sydney we should not attend the gala to honor Dad. The last thing I want to do is bring this ugliness to something he's worked so hard for—"

"That's absolute nonsense. Your father would be devastated if his only child were not present to celebrate him."

Donathan had spoken to his father briefly and as usual he had been so optimistic, telling Donathan life lessons were hard, but this too shall pass. He looked at his mother and committed this instance to memory. It was a rare occasion that both Sylver and Sydney agreed on anything.

"Here," his mother said, softening her tone and handing him a business card. "Rebecca is brilliant, trustworthy, and a very good friend. I've briefed her on the situation, and she's expecting your call."

CHAPTER 16

Avoiding a few bicyclists, Sydney James maneuvered her Range Rover up the winding road toward Tilden Regional Park. She stopped at the clearing to marvel at the breathtaking views of the San Francisco Bay and the infamous Golden Gate Bridge.

She had taken this drive many times before, and every time it was like witnessing this sweeping beauty for the first time. She took a deep breath.

Sydney sighed, and then second-guessed her decision to do a group run with Black Girls Run this morning. She really wasn't in the mood for idle chitchat. What she needed was a long solo run so her mind could problem-solve and put her life in order. But she'd made the commitment, so she reached for her door handle, got back into her truck, and continued toward the merry-go-round meeting point.

The deeper she drove into the park, the thicker the fog became, which heightened Sydney's anxiety. She had never been to this part of the park before, and after driving around for about fifteen minutes, she found herself on a one-way service road and decided she was headed in the wrong direction.

When she turned around, she came upon a brown building and turned into the parking lot. There were no other vehicles in the lot, so she drove parallel with the building, craning her neck for any sign of life before she decided to park and get out. She noticed a kiosk a few feet up the road, and she began a brisk jog in that direction.

After running a few yards, Sydney heard a crackling noise and paused, unsure where it was coming from. For the first time, the seriousness of her situation paralyzed her. What the hell was she thinking wandering around this deserted park alone this time of the morning? This wasn't safe. By the time she reached the stand, she was in her head, psyching herself up. Her eyes darted around the Plexiglas, trying to make sense of the map in front of her, but now her nerves were in overdrive. She kept reminding herself that she was overreacting, and the sounds she heard had nothing to do with some animal—or with Austyn Greene.

"Are you lost?" a woman's voice said.

Sydney's breath caught in her chest, and her hands balled into fists at her side. Heart racing, she pivoted to face the voice coming from behind her. When Sydney made eye contact with the raven-haired woman, her body relaxed.

The woman was wearing running shoes, tights, and a Cal Berkeley sweatshirt.

"Are you lost?" the woman asked again.

"I'm afraid so. I was meeting my running group at the merry-go-round, and I somehow got turned around."

"The carousel is located on the other side of the park. You have to go in on the Orinda side."

"Can I get there from here?"

"Well, actually the quickest way is to go back out of the park, get on Highway Twenty-Four, and take the Orinda exit."

"Thank you. You're a lifesaver."

"You're welcome," she said, and then ran off in the direction of the one-way service road.

Locked inside the confines of her car, Sydney breathed normally again. Calming herself, she drew in and released several long breaths. She picked up her iPhone from the passenger seat to call the run leader, but there was no service.

"Damn," she mumbled.

She'd had enough of this craziness, but her mind was wound up pretty tight and running helped her think. These days she had no idea what she'd get from Donathan. One minute he was fine, and the next they were having outrageous arguments about nothing. After his blowup at dinner, he flat-out told her that he could never accept another man pleasuring his woman. With the help of a therapist, she had contemplated telling him about her indiscretion with Miles, but there was no way she could do that now. Then and there, Sydney made a decision: Shrink or no shrink, she had way too much to lose if Donathan ever found out about her and Miles. He would never be able to forgive her.

CHAPTER 17

Not sure exactly what it was that he was looking for, Donathan circled the property until he noticed the yellow crime scene tape covering one of the doors, then parked his car. He'd promised Sydney that he would let the police do their job, yet here he was parked outside the Motel 6 in Pleasanton. He surveyed the outdoor walkways leading to the rooms, trying to imagine the route the killer had taken. No word from Holsey again, but he also believed this situation had Austyn Greene written all over it.

He noticed two balding white men exiting the double doors. Their cheap suits and protruding guts screamed police who spent way too much time sitting at a desk instead of fighting crime. He'd done some research and learned that Pleasanton hadn't had a homicide in over five years, which meant these guys were just a little bit rusty, to say the least.

A news truck with KTVU Channel 2 plastered on its side turned into the parking lot and caught his attention.

"Shit," he mumbled, slipping his shades on and scooting down in his seat. His windows were tinted, but the last thing he needed was to be seen here by a reporter. When he became a regular on the KBLX morning radio show, he became an instant media darling. His face was plastered on billboards, bus stops, and all over the radio station's social media pages. To the chagrin of his mother, the "Sex Doctor" was everywhere. His rise to fame had been on his terms, and it was great. But as soon as those pictures of him kissing Austyn hit the web, he became a condemned man.

It was like the media wanted him to fail, and no matter what he said, they continued printing that filth because filth sells. It had only been a few days since he'd had the impromptu press conference outside his house that had gotten the vultures off his back, but if they caught him here at this murder scene, they would be back to making his life impossible. And if they did that, his mother would absolutely kill him.

Sydney had finally talked him into attending the recognition dinner for his father, even though he still had his concerns. His father, Dr. Maurice James, worked hard and deserved any award being presented to him. The last thing Donathan wanted to do was to mess it up for him.

He sank down deeper into the plush leather seat, and the passenger car door jerked open. Donathan's back straightened to an upright position.

"What the hell—?"

Before he could get out another word, Payton slid into the passenger seat and closed the door behind her.

"Are you following me?" he accused.

"What?"

"Did Sydney put you up to this?"

"Sydney? Donathan, you are seriously tripping."

"Then who?"

Donathan flashed Payton a look that said, *You better start talking.*

With Payton showing up here, he was beginning to believe that being here was a mistake. He gave her a cold, hard stare as he waited for an answer. Her normally natural hair had been straightened and was styled into a bob with swoop bangs that covered her face from his view. She was avoiding eye contact and seemed to be at a loss for words—all insecure behavior he had never seen from her. She was one of the most overconfident people that he knew. The psychologist in him and expert at reading behavior and body language always knew there was something behind Payton's bravado. But it would have been inappropriate for her to be his patient so it wasn't his place to diagnose her ills. She finally looked at him.

"I saw the story on the news, and I was curious—"

"C'mon, Payton. You expect me to believe that you saw a story on the news and decided to just show up at the scene of the crime?"

The murder count in Oakland was through the roof, but this single unsolved murder in suburbia had taken top billing on all the news channels in the Bay Area. Unlike crime in urban communities, there was something just a little sexier about crime in the middle of the suburbs. So her seeing the story on TV was plausible, but there was more to what actually brought her here. And that more was Sydney.

"Cut the bullshit, Payton. I know Sydney put you up to this, and I don't appreciate her having me followed. I'm a grown-ass man."

"Look, Donathan. Sydney had nothing to do with the reason I'm here. I came here looking for some answers."

"What kind of answers?"

Payton looked away, avoiding eye contact.

"I think the woman who is castrating these men is my half sister."

"What?!" Donathan said, confused by what she was saying. He had known Payton for years, but never knew her to have any siblings. He searched his memory for what he actually knew about his wife's best friend. Payton grew up in Pittsburg and was raised by her grandparents. He had never heard of her having any siblings. She attended UCLA, which was where she and Sydney met.

As if reading his mind, Payton continued, "I don't know for sure, but that's what I'm trying to figure out."

"But you don't have any sisters."

"None that I know of, but a few weeks ago, after the pictures of you and Austyn Greene were plastered all over the internet, she showed up at my grandparents' home in Pittsburg looking for my mother. I couldn't place her face initially, but by the time she left I was sure she was the same woman in those pictures on the internet with you."

"What did she want with your mother?"

"That's just it. I have no clue. It was like coming face-to-face with the dead that I would rather stay buried. Lois has not lived in Pittsburg in over twenty-five years. When I asked Austyn what she wanted, she was very vague in a rude kind of way. I've racked my brain trying to figure out what the hell anybody would want with the likes of Lois Greene, but I—"

Donathan looked around expecting someone else to show up, hop in the car, and tell him he was on one of those practical joke reality shows. If Payton and Austyn were sisters, what exactly did that mean? He was almost afraid to ask the next question.

"Let me get this straight. Are you saying that Lois Greene is your mother?"

"Well, I'd prefer that you didn't call the bitch who abandoned me my mother, but yeah, she did give birth to me."

Donathan was stunned. One minute he'd hired Holsey Investigations to track Lois down, but now the key that could lead him right to her and Austyn Greene was sitting across from him in his passenger seat.

"Do you know where Lois is?"

"Not really. I mean, I'm not sure. Last I'd heard she was in Los Angeles, but lately, my uncle keeps alluding to the fact that she's back in Pittsburg."

"Do you believe him?"

"At first I thought it was just a coincidence, but the last time I saw him, he was pretty convincing."

"Can you get him to take you to her?"

"We aren't on the best of terms right now, but I'm headed out to Pittsburg to check on him."

"Look, Payton. All bullshit aside. We need to locate Lois."

"I thought this was about Austyn?"

"It is, but if I find Lois, then I'm sure I'll find Austyn."

"And what makes you so sure of that? Austyn doesn't even

look like Lois, and so what if both their last names are Greene. So are a lot of other people's."

"Because the last time I saw Austyn, she told me that she was going to kill me and her mother, Lois Greene, and I believe her."

Payton leaned back in the passenger seat, and an uncomfortable expression washed over her face.

"I need your help."

She shot a quick glance at Donathan. "Help to do what?"

"Find your mother—"

"There is no way in hell I'm looking for that woman! And don't call her my mother. Most people care about their mothers, and I don't give a damn if that bitch gets hit by a Mack truck!"

"Calm down, Payton. All I want you to do is talk to your uncle to see if you can get him to tell you Lois's whereabouts."

"I'll see what I can do, but I can't promise anything. He has a serious drug problem and to say he's not thinking clearly right now is an understatement."

"Understood. I just want all of us to be safe, but we have to put Austyn where she belongs to do that."

After Payton drove out of the parking lot, Donathan noticed a security camera like the one he had at his office mounted to the upper corner of the redbrick building across the parking lot. From the mounted angle, if whoever killed the victim exited on this side of the building, then he was sure the camera would have captured their image. He looked around for any signs of the media or police before he started the ignition and drove the short distance to the building. He didn't know how he was going to talk them into letting him see the footage, but he had to at least try.

Taking long, deliberate strides, Donathan tossed different scenarios around in his head as he approached the glass doors. He hoped the camera wasn't being used as a deterrent and had actually been recording a few nights ago. When he entered the double doors, a security guard sitting at the front desk greeted him.

"Detective Allen, right?" the guard said, reaching across the desk.

"Good afternoon." Donathan nodded, offering him a firm handshake, but choosing not to correct the man on his identity.

"Man, you're quick. Wait right here, and I'll grab the copy of that camera footage for you."

Donathan looked on as the security guard trotted down the hallway and disappeared behind a closed door. In his mind he struggled with coming clean about who he really was. He could get into so much trouble for tampering with a police investigation, but his life was in danger and he needed to take a quick look at the video for himself. Once he did, he would find Detective Allen and make sure he received the tape.

"I still can't believe someone got murdered," the guard said, coming toward him with a large white business envelope.

"Yeah, it is pretty unbelievable for Pleasanton," Donathan said, really looking at the man for the first time. His name tag read *Walter*, and his jet-black hair looked unnatural, like he'd given himself a bad dye job.

"We made a copy of the video feed for the past few days like you requested. I also placed my card inside the envelope in case you need anything else."

Donathan nodded and shook hands with the man a second time, then hurried from the building. As he eased behind the wheel of the car, he experienced a moment of deep satisfaction. A few days ago finding Austyn seemed like an uphill battle, but things were looking much better now. Weeks of wondering where Austyn Greene had vanished to would become clearer once he viewed the tape.

CHAPTER 18

Tony held the receiver and listened as his aunt Rosemary spouted off unsolicited parenting advice. His insides were knotted, and after a sleepless night, his patience was thin. Najee was determined to be independent. Berkeley was one thing, but did she possess the street smarts to run around the mean streets of Oakland without supervision? It was his job to keep her safe. How was he going to protect her?

"You have to let the girl breathe," his aunt informed him. "She's a good girl, and she makes good decisions."

"It's not her decisions I'm afraid of."

"I know you're scared, baby, but you have to let her make her own mistakes and learn from them."

After ending the call, he sat at the breakfast bar ruminating on his aunt's last words. Maybe she was right. Najee deserved much more credit than he gave her. Sure, there was a difference between Oakland and Berkeley, but the one constant was street smarts, which were required if she lived in either city.

He went to her slightly ajar bedroom door, then knocked lightly before going inside.

"Naj," he called softly to the mass hidden by the purple and green comforter pulled up over her head.

It didn't matter if he was in denial or not. She was sixteen and closer to adulthood than the little eight-year-old girl he used to take to Fentons for a scoop of bubblegum ice cream. He chuckled at the memory of her talking his ear off and absentmindedly picking out each ball of sugar to chew at the end. He smiled at the sleeping beauty peeking at him from squinted eyes.

"What time is it?"

"Almost seven."

"Oh, Gaaawwwwd," she grumbled. "Haven't you heard of summertime?"

He yanked off the bedding and tickled her like he used to do when she was younger.

"Stop it! Please stop it." She squirmed and giggled.

"I'm about to head out for work."

"Please tell me that I do not have to go to your friend's house."

"No. I'm going to let you stay here."

Najee jumped up, wrapped her arms around his neck, and kissed his cheek over and over again.

"But here are the rules. When you are not home, I need to know exactly who you are with, where you are going, when precisely I should expect you home, and what you will be doing. I'm not happy about you riding in cars with other teenage drivers, but until I can teach you how to drive and get you a car of your own, I'll do my best to live with it."

"Is that it?" she asked, the statement laced with sarcasm.

"No, it's not. I don't want any boys in the house when I'm not home, nor are you allowed to be in anyone else's house with boys without adult supervision. On weekdays your curfew is nine o'clock and on the weekends ten o'clock."

"Curfew? This is a joke, right? Mom never gave me a curfew. I'm going into the eleventh grade, for Christ's sake!"

He flashed her a stern look. "I'm not Mom, and we can talk more about it later."

The bedroom door closed, and tears immediately sprang from Najee's eyes. She fell back onto the bed, curled into a sobbing ball, and grieved for her freedom with each tear that rolled down her cheek. She didn't understand why he was treating her like she was a child. She wanted her old life back. She wanted to go home. She wanted her mama.

Long after Najee heard the truck pull out of the driveway, she texted her friend Lauren an ambulance emoji, their signal for 911, to call back, and her cell phone began to ring almost immediately. She answered the phone without looking at the screen.

"Hello."

"What's wrong?"

"My life is over!"

"Uhm, what exactly does that mean?"

"He gave me a curfew! And a laundry list of things I have to do before I can step foot outside this prison."

"Quit being so dramatic. I'm sure it can't be that bad."

"You have no idea."

"Actually, I do. I have a curfew."

"What? Why is this the first time I'm hearing about it?"

"Look, after I take my little brother to soccer camp at eleven, I'll swoop you up and we can go to the movies and hang out on Bay Street. I'll call you when I'm on the way?"

"Okay, I'll see you then."

Najee hung up the phone and started a text to Tony, but then quickly changed her mind. She wasn't a kid, and it was broad daylight. She was responsible enough to hang out with her friends and be back home before he returned from work.

CHAPTER 19

Austyn took a second look at the unfamiliar image reflected back at her in the dust-hazed mirror. Her hair was a mass of long blond braids, and her lips were smeared with black-cherry lipstick, a color she'd never be caught dead in under normal circumstances. No one would recognize her as the woman wanted for questioning related to the Donathan and Sydney James debacle and for killing a bunch of worthless bastards. She was so close to finding Lois Greene, and this little disguise was going to lead her right to her mother.

Yesterday, she called the telephone number listed on the Glover House website to inquire about volunteer opportunities. After a lengthy telephone conversation with a staff person who answered the phone, Austyn learned that Glover House didn't accept volunteers. However, the woman did recommend Loaves and Fishes as a great place for charity work. In fact, she went on to say, volunteerism was a huge part of the Glover House recovery philosophy, and all the women in treatment volunteered.

Immediately, Austyn ended the call and typed *Loaves and Fishes* into the search bar on her computer. She filled out a volunteer application online, checked a few boxes, and within hours received a phone call to schedule an appointment with the manager. If she couldn't get to Lois inside, then she'd let Lois come to her outside, and this was the day.

★ ★ ★

Twenty minutes later, Austyn took a seat on an empty bench outside the administration offices at the food program. She studied the groups of people going in and out of the soup kitchen and focused her attention on a mother holding the hand of a young child. When the mother released the child's hand to retrieve something from her backpack, the little girl wrapped her arms around the woman's waist and held on tight as if her mother was her protector. Austyn searched the crevices of her mind, but she could never remember a time when her mother ever held her hand like that.

As she painted the vivid pictures in her mind, a tool she learned in therapy, she could see images of Lois Greene's harsh face and every one of those filthy bastards who stole her innocence, including the gang members in Los Angeles who kept her locked in the basement for days, raping her repeatedly before beating her unconscious and leaving her for dead. She woke up from the ordeal alone in a deserted lot in South Central Los Angeles. When she mustered the strength to move, she walked for what seemed like miles before someone stopped to help her. The police questioned her continually, but she told them she didn't remember anything, and soon the questions stopped. Then payback became her obsession.

She returned to her life and began the physical healing process, but mentally, she never forgot. And when the time was right, her revenge took her back to South Central, and she found them all existing not far from where they'd raped her. She stalked them, then, using what they took from her, lured them in one by one and made them pay.

A short, stubby man standing in one of the office doorways called out to her, interrupting her thoughts.

"Hellooooo. I said, may I help you?" His tone was a harsh demand.

Austyn placed her hand in the pocket of her jean jacket and

wrapped it around the cold stainless-steel handle before she made eye contact with him.

"I'm here to meet with Roberta Clayborne about volunteering."

"Roberta is out sick today. My name is Stanley Mason. I'll be doing your intake and giving you an overview of the program and the tour. C'mon, this way," he said in a no-nonsense kind of way. He turned his back to her and took quick, hurried steps down a narrow hallway.

"I don't know what you did to be mandated to volunteer, but we don't stand for no foolishness around here, and we treat people with respect. And if Roberta assigns you to my kitchen, you gon' have to do something with that hair."

The man placed her in an empty room with a yellow number 2 pencil and a five-page questionnaire. After spending twenty minutes taking the assessment, he gave Austyn an overview of the Loaves and Fishes program, and ended with a tour of the facility. The last stop on the tour was a work schedule posted on the wall in the kitchen. It listed volunteers by first name only and the hours and jobs they were assigned at the facility. She quickly scrolled down the list, but didn't see the name she was looking for or any reference to Glover House.

"Do women from the Glover House treatment home volunteer here?"

The man spun around so quickly, Austyn could almost taste the onions and garlic he had for lunch. He narrowed his eyes and leaned in close before he spoke. "Who does and does not volunteer here is of no concern to you. The only name you need to be looking for on the list is yours. Now, pay attention to what I'm telling you, or we won't be needing your services. Are we clear?"

"Crystal," she said, holding his eye contact and tossing her long golden braids over her shoulder.

★　★　★

Austyn left Loaves and Fishes, a hostage to her thoughts. Did the Glover House women volunteer there, or was she wasting her time? She didn't notice the lights and sirens in her rearview mirror until the Pittsburg police officer was on her bumper. She checked the odometer and panicked.

She raked the braids on the wig forward with her hand to cover her face, then inched her skirt up to rest high on her thighs before pulling to the shoulder. She kept her eyes glued to the rearview mirror, watching the officer step out of the black and white vehicle and make his way toward her.

"Stay calm, stay calm," she mumbled.

By the time he made it to the driver's-side window, pure adrenaline was seeping from her pores. She avoided his eyes, but his voice was stern and no-nonsense.

"License and registration, please."

Austyn leaned over and fumbled in the glove box. "Did I do something wrong, Officer?"

She retrieved the fake driver's license and registration she'd acquired after she purchased the car, and with her hand shaking she handed him the documents.

He stepped back, gave the car a quick once-over as he reviewed the documents.

"Los Angeles? You're a long way from home."

"I'm really sorry, Officer," she said, squeezing her thighs together, making her skirt rise even higher. "Was I speeding?"

The officer ignored her chitchat, and was unfazed by her attempts to exploit her femininity.

"I'll be right back."

Austyn kept her head down. She could feel a blanket of perspiration rolling down her back. She imagined there was a Most Wanted picture of her taped to the dashboard, and a police officer running her real name through the database. She couldn't let this happen. She was too close to Lois, and she needed to finish what she started. Her eyes darted to the on-ramp at the next intersection. If she maneuvered onto the highway, she'd be exposed from too many angles and the law would apprehend her in no time. So, caught up in devising her escape plan, she didn't notice the officer standing back at her window. He handed the driver's license and car registration back to her.

"Ma'am, one of your taillights is blown out. I'm going to let you go with a warning this time, but you need to get it fixed immediately."

"Thank you, Officer. I promise to take care of the taillight first thing in the morning."

The police cruiser pulled into traffic, and Austyn blew out a ragged sigh and rested her head on the steering wheel. That was too close for comfort. Way too close.

CHAPTER 20

After sitting in nauseating stop-and-go traffic for over an hour, Payton parallel-parked next to the curb of Lake Chalet Seafood Bar and Grill. She needed a drink. The beautifully revived historical building was nestled along Oakland's Lake Merritt and reminded her of an old California mission.

Lake Chalet's main clientele were city politician types doing table business, and the Oakland set who appreciated the picturesque windows with spectacular views of the lake.

Payton hoped a few glasses of wine would suffocate her frustrations. She'd reached out to her uncle Sheldon for the umpteenth time without response. Where the hell was he? She began to get worried. He had gone off the grid before, but something in her gut told her this time was different. Maybe it was all the talk about Lois Greene and Austyn.

Payton dialed Sheldon's number again, this time with the intent to leave him a voice mail. As she waited for the greeting to end, Payton's thoughts raced back to the Motel 6 in Pleasanton. She couldn't believe Austyn Greene, the lunatic bitch who was terrorizing the city, was her half sister. Hell, who was she kidding? It was her suspicions of this very fact that caused her to drive out to Pleasanton in the first place. She spoke in a hushed tone into the receiver.

"Uncle Sheldon, this is serious. I've called you several times, and I need you to call me back as soon as you get this message." She pressed the red icon on the iPhone screen. Stepping up to the patio bar, she announced, "I'll have a glass of the P. Harrell 'Haight Street' Riesling."

Glass in hand, Payton walked along the length of the dock, wrestling with her feelings. She took a seat on the resin wicker love seat closest to the water and tried to repress them, before downing the contents of her glass in one continuous gulp. On so many levels, she felt sorry for Austyn, because she knew that Lois Greene fucked up everything she touched. On the other hand, Austyn was dangerous and had hurt people whom Payton loved.

When Payton turned to motion for the waiter to order another drink, she did a double take at the sight of a woman coming down the extended pier toward her. She'd seen many pictures of Celestine and David Bryant online and in the social pages of the local paper, had even breathed the same air with her at a few charity functions. But the two women had never been formally introduced. Normally, Celestine, who was an entertainment attorney, was the picture of power or glamour, depending on the occasion. Perfect hair, power suits, or ball gowns and diamonds draped at her throat.

Today, she wore a charcoal-gray maxi sweater that flared above her black skinny jeans and a black Golden State Warriors "The City" T-shirt covered with rhinestones and crystals. A pair of black strappy sandals, crisscrossed around her ankles, punctuated the casual yet chic look that many high-powered women coveted but couldn't pull off.

Payton took a quick glance at the dark, shimmering waters of the lake. There was no need to panic. Her rule of thumb was never to discuss her bedroom antics with acquaintances, especially when they were the wives of the men who partook in those bedroom antics with her.

Before Celestine reached the love seat, she stopped at a nearby table, dusted off the burnt-orange seat cushion, and took a seat.

She removed a small silver compact from her oversized designer tote bag and studied her reflection. Payton glanced away, happy there would be no undignified confrontation today. She simply wasn't in the mood.

"I was beginning to think you were avoiding me."

Payton whipped her head around at the sound of Celestine's voice. A young man, whom Payton knew to be Celestine and David's son, joined his mother at the table.

DeMarcus Bryant was well over six feet tall, in his early thirties, and extremely good-looking by any woman's standards. With meticulously cropped hair, dark eyes, and well-balanced facial features, he was the spitting image of his father, only a few shades darker. And not only was he good-looking, but his money made him a double threat, which meant a constant flow of thirsty women was hoping to become his flavor of the month. He kissed his mother on the cheek and placed two cocktails on the table.

"Ma, it's not even like that. With Dad giving me more responsibility at the downtown dealership, I'm extremely busy, and when I'm not working, I'm spending time with Chanelle."

"How is my grandbaby anyway?"

"She's fine."

"And the situation with her mother?"

DeMarcus laughed. "Ma, are you serious? You slapped every child custody injunction on that woman the court would allow."

"Well, I just want what's best for my grandbaby. I don't want her to be used for greed or as some kind of custody pawn."

Overwhelmed by the Bryant family's lively conversation, Payton gazed at the authentic Venetian gondola gliding across the still water, then stared at her now-empty wineglass. Unable to relax, she motioned for the waiter, and for the first time made eye contact with DeMarcus.

Once or twice, they'd encountered one another at the dealership when she stopped by for a meeting with David. Her visits were strictly for professional reasons, nothing that divulged she and his father were bed buddies and fucked every chance they got.

DeMarcus leaned back in his chair, crossed one leg over the other, and took a hearty sip of the deep copper liquid that filled his glass. His distrustful eyes held her gaze, as he asked Celestine, "Is Dad on his way?"

"Yes, love. He said he'd be here in about fifteen minutes."

Payton took that tidbit of information as her cue to leave. Of all the restaurants in the city of Oakland, why did the Bryant family have to choose the one across the street from her condo for their little family reunion this evening? She grabbed her handbag and sashayed toward the exit, her eyes again locking with DeMarcus as she passed by the table. This time an inviting sneer crossed his lips.

"DeMarcus! Quit staring. It's rude. I raised you better than that. I mean, she's cute, but just a tad bit old for you. More of your father's type."

Payton paused mentally but her feet kept moving. Did that bitch just say she was too old? Well, Celestine was right about one thing. Her husband, David, sniffed at this "old" ass every chance he got.

An air-conditioned breeze escaped through the restaurant doors, bringing with it the smell of mouthwatering seafood. Payton walked up to the main bar and took a seat a few stools away from David, who'd just stepped up to the bar. He was fit for a man in his early sixties, and the tailor-made suit hugged his frame perfectly like a second skin, a DILF (Dad I'd Love to Fuck) by anybody's standards. He adjusted his necktie, and the simple gesture unleashed a flood of butterflies in the pit of her stomach. She could almost feel the handmade silk with beautiful detail looped around her wrist . . . something David loved to do. For a quick second she wanted to smile, but then she remembered she was pissed by the impromptu Bryant family reunion invading her lakeside sanctuary. David ordered his standard, Casa Dragones, a sipping tequila, before the bartender made his way to her. "What can I get for you, beautiful?" the bartender asked.

"I'll take a bottle of the P. Harrell 'Haight Street' Riesling to go and put it on his tab," she said, gesturing in David's direction.

"Well, let's make sure that's okay with the gentleman."

David nodded for confirmation but avoided looking in the direction of the familiar voice coming from the other end of the bar. The bartender stepped away, and within minutes returned with the wine Payton requested sealed in a to-go wine bag, as required by law.

"Save a glass for me," he said as if talking to no one in particular.

Payton laughed weakly. Usually a bottle of wine would last her a few days, but this bottle would be empty by night's end. She tucked the wine bag under her arm and stood up to leave.

"Your family is seated on the dock. And I'm sure you'll find it interesting to know that wifey thinks I'm cute, and even though I'm too old for your son, according to her, I'm just your type."

"Payton, you didn't—" he said, looking at her for the first time.

And she knew right away who she was dealing with. This was not the man who brazenly fed her in public. This was the dude who acted like he would be condemned guilty of some phantom shit simply because he knew her. A complexity of David Bryant she never quite understood but was quickly growing tired of.

"Now, you know better than that. Your secrets will always be safe with me," she said, her voice trailing off as she made her way toward the front door. Once she reached the exit, she glanced back, and just as she thought his eyes were fixated on her ass like glue, she winked.

"Nice tie."

Less than five minutes later, Payton pulled into her reserved parking space in the underground garage of the luxury high-rise condos across the street. Once inside her building, she decided she was too wound up and needed to exert some of her pent-up energy before uncorking her bottle of wine.

The gym at Essex was deserted, so she hurried upstairs, changed into her workout clothes, and quickly made her way back down-stairs. Next time she saw David, she would make it a point to let him know that Lake Chalet was her territory, and his family ren-dezvous were not welcomed there.

An hour later, Payton stepped off the treadmill, gasping for breath, her mind preoccupied with the physical sensations in her glutes, hamstrings, and quads. A reprieve from the unfamiliar sen-sations squeezing her heart. Feelings were the enemy. She didn't want to feel. But when Tony came to mind, her resolve vanished. She took out her phone and checked for missed messages.

There was one. As she pressed in her password and waited for the message to play back, she prayed it was from Tony. She could really use his smart thinking right now.

"Hello, Ms. Jones. This is Brandy from Brown and Franklin Real Estate Investments. We found a few boxes in the attic of the Pittsburg property, and I'd like to get them to you. I'll be here today and tomorrow until five p.m., and you can stop by and pick them up. Otherwise, give me a call to schedule another time."

Payton glanced at her watch. It was already past five o'clock, but the phone call was a sign she needed to take her ass to Pitts-burg. Though the trip would have to wait until tomorrow, be-cause the only thing on her to-do list this evening was the bottle of wine chilling in the fridge and the recorded shows on her DVR. In the morning, after a good night's rest, she would be bet-ter equipped to deal with her uncle Sheldon.

She fired off a text.

I'm coming to Pittsburg first thing in the morning. Be in your room. It's important.

CHAPTER 21

The wheels of the plane touched down in Oakland and jarred Miles Day from a restless slumber. Due to a global computer glitch, he'd spent well over six hours at O'Hare International waiting for his flight to depart. During the delay, he read numerous stories on his iPad about the thousands of passengers stranded in airports worldwide, and right now, with the wheels down, he was glad to be home.

Fourteen days, and he could not wait to lie in his own bed and smother his head in his own pillows. He searched his memory. Even though the South Side of Chicago would forever course through his veins, this was the first time he could remember thinking of Oakland as home since he'd moved here a few months ago.

As the plane taxied toward the gate, Miles opened his eyes and squinted, adjusting to the now-bright overhead cabin lighting. He powered up his cell phone to call for car service, then quickly changed his mind. In the time it would take for them to send a sedan, he could have hailed a taxi and been pulling up to his front door.

He glanced at his calendar. Tomorrow he was due at the hospital bright and early, then home in enough time to read a goodnight story to Arielle and Lauren via FaceTime. The thought of his daughters made Miles smile. Over the past two weeks, he'd spent every moment he could with them. Yet, his heart ached at the thought of what him being divorced and living in another state would do to them.

The plane barely came to a complete stop before Miles stood with his leather backpack slung across his shoulder and retrieved his carry-on luggage from the overhead compartment.

"Mr. Day, here are your items," the flight attendant said, handing him the inconspicuous black garment bag.

"Thank you." He smiled and folded the attire across his forearm, eager to escape the confined space.

When the doors opened, Miles hurried up the jetway and through the deserted terminal. Once outside, he moved with intention toward the taxi curbside pickup of Terminal 1. He shoved his luggage and backpack in the back seat of the cab, then folded his over-six-foot frame into the tight confines of the back seat, second-guessing his decision not to phone for car service.

"Jack London Square, corner of Broadway and Second Street."

It was late, no traffic, and the ride downtown would be over in no time as long as the Black Lives Matter protesters hadn't taken over the freeway or blocked traffic on Broadway. He, too, was outraged that black men were being murdered in this country with no accountability, and even though he didn't have the answers, something had to be done.

Miles turned his attention to the digital taxi display. Like a tourist, he mindlessly viewed news clips and a few restaurant promotions. But what he saw next made him want to put his fist through the small LCD screen. Donathan James was promoting the local morning radio show. Seeing his face brought back a rush of memories for Miles.

He despised the arrogant mothafucker. If only Miles had the foresight to maintain his composure that day instead of making a complete fool of himself fist-fighting another grown-ass man. And in front of so many of his colleagues. Those were the ramifications he would have to live with, but truth be told, the images of Donathan conjured up something else. Sydney James. No matter how much he tried not to think about her, she kept pushing her way into his mind. During his self-imposed exile to Chicago, Sydney reached out to him numerous times, and it took tremendous willpower not to respond to her attempts at contacting him. What he needed to say to her would be done face-to-face, not via text or cell phone.

Miles was smart enough to know the consequences of coming between a man and his wife, and that was the reason he'd fled to Chicago—to get his mind right. But before he stepped foot on the plane to return to Oakland, he decided that he was done pretending that nothing happened between them. He wanted her.

What did Sydney see in that dude? It was painfully obvious that Donathan James was a fucking idiot. What married man would let his wife shack up in a hotel for days without bothering to check up on her? Donathan James personified a poor excuse for a husband. It was men like him who didn't miss a good thing until it was no longer sleeping next to him. Probably a side effect of being born with a silver spoon in his mouth. Point-blank, Miles was there for Sydney at a time when she needed a friend, and he didn't give a damn what Donathan thought about it.

But who was he kidding? If he was being honest, his attraction to Sydney began the moment he was introduced to her as his colleague. He'd broken the family motto he shared with his brothers: *Never fuck with married pussy.* They were words to live by, but he crossed the line that night at the Waterfront Hotel and there was no turning back.

He couldn't remember ever wanting a woman this much, not even his ex-wife, Stephanie. A fleeting thought passed through his mind and lingered. He remembered how he palmed Sydney's ass and teased the clean-shaven flesh between her legs. His reward and punishment, her sweet juices on the tip of his tongue. Once he tasted her, the realization of what was happening slapped him in the face. Even though Sydney was the initiator, she was drunk, and the last thing he wanted or needed was for her to wake up with regrets. He promised her in that moment that if and when he ever pleasured her again, it would be because she wanted him to, not because she had too much to drink or because she was mad at her husband. Now he was back and armed with his motive to make good on that promise.

The yellow cab came to a stop in front of the Ellington luxury full-service high-rise. Before Miles could open the car door, he was greeted by the on-staff security guard, who opened the door closest to the curb.

"Welcome home, Mr. Day. May I take your luggage?"

Miles hesitated, then allowed the young man to retrieve his bags.

"Thanks, Calvin. You can take it right up and leave it by the door."

"Will you be needing anything else this evening?"

"Nope. Just my bed."

Living in a luxury condo with around-the-clock staff to respond to his every need still took some getting used to. He paid a handsome homeowners' association fee for the convenience of a pool, gym, and personal assistant/concierge. It wasn't a great place for kids, but since his daughters were four and six years old, he'd be the one doing the traveling back and forth to spend time with them. This was perfect for now.

Miles followed behind the security guard as he stepped inside the elevator and hit the button for the fourteenth floor. He glanced at his watch. By the time he showered and made it to bed, he'd be lucky if he got four good hours of sleep tonight, but as a doctor, he'd survived with far less. Besides, his adrenaline would sustain him. No need to rush or go in like a bull in a china shop. He knew exactly what he wanted, and just like the first time, he knew exactly how to be patient until he got it.

CHAPTER 22

"C'mon, Najee, it won't hurt you," Lauren and Samantha both pressed. "You need to relax," Samantha said as all three girls sat cross-legged on Lauren's bedroom floor. Najee stood up.

"Drugs?" Najee questioned. "Where did you get this?"

"I got it from my dad's desk drawer, and weed is not a real drug. I mean, it's practically legal." Samantha pushed the joint in Najee's direction.

Taking her eyes off the joint for one quick second, Najee shot Lauren a questioning look, but she quickly turned her gaze away.

"Here," Samantha pressed again.

Najee had never smoked weed or taken any kind of drugs in her life, and she hated being pressured into doing it now. But she didn't want to be labeled as the not-cool girl either. She and Lauren had been best friends since elementary school. Drugs weren't their thing. They hung out, went to the movies, and shopped like crazy, but they didn't do drugs. Samantha, on the other hand, was new to Lauren's neighborhood and clearly a bad influence. Her family moved in at the end of the school year, and it was like she and Lauren were becoming best friends. Najee reached for the joint, took a quick puff, and slowly blew the smoke out of her mouth, careful not to inhale the visible haze into her lungs. She handed it back.

"Now, that wasn't so bad." Samantha grinned.

"Are we going to Bay Street?" Najee asked as she flopped down on Lauren's unmade bed and began picking at her fuchsia nail polish.

Samantha responded, "Yeah, we are, but first let's enjoy the high."

A few hours later, Najee sat in silence in the back seat as Lauren drove toward the outdoor mall. For the past few months, she tried to find reasons to like Samantha, but there was something about her that just didn't feel right. And why was she the boss of everything all of a sudden? Probably the number-one reason nobody at school liked her.

Samantha was tall and skinny, but it was her pale-white skin and medium-length hair dyed jet black that made her stand out in the crowd. Najee didn't know much about her, except she always complained about her controlling father, who made things miserable for her at home.

They pulled into the parking garage and parked on the second level closest to the movie theater. Lauren made eye contact with Najee in the rearview mirror, her light brown eyes red and glassy.

"We don't have time for the movie today, but I thought we could grab a quick bite to eat and hit a few stores to get a new outfit for Blue's party."

"Cool. I need to pick up a book from Barnes and Noble for—"

"Book? I swear, you are such a nerd," Samantha teased.

Lauren let out a lazy giggle. "Samantha, I bet you don't even read."

Najee decided then and there this would be the last time she hung out with Samantha. If Lauren wanted to be her friend, that was her prerogative, but as far as Najee was concerned, Samantha was a loser. They were sixteen years old, heading into their junior year of high school. It was time to narrow down which colleges they wanted to attend, not get derailed by some pothead.

Her brother worked hard, but he had never gone to college, or at least that's what she thought. The other day, while organizing mail on the counter, Najee found a letter from California State East Bay. At first, she thought it was college mail for her, but the opened letter was addressed to Tony. It said he was granted the *Incomplete* from the class and all he needed to do was take the final exam to obtain his bachelor's degree. That was pretty cool. She remembered her mother always saying how proud she was of him. How he made his own way, but she would be even prouder now.

She hated cancer. She missed her mom.

Once she and Tony were on speaking terms again, maybe she would share with him that she was proud of him, too. But first he had to stop treating her like she was a baby and stop keeping her locked up like a prisoner. She deserved to make her own way, too.

"C'mon, Na...jee." Samantha dragged out her name, overexaggerating the two syllables.

"You are so childish," Najee snapped back. "Lauren, I'm going to Barnes and Noble, I'll catch up with you and your obnoxious-ass friend later."

"C'mon, Naj. She was only kidding."

"Look at you making excuses for her and talking like she's not standing right there." Najee's eyes welled up with tears. "I'm done dealing with this."

"She's just overreacting because her mother died."

"Damn, Samantha, I can't believe you said that! Najee, wait," Lauren called after her. "How are you getting home?"

"Uber!"

Before Lauren could catch up to her, Najee dashed into the bookstore. She didn't know whom she was more upset with: Lauren, Samantha, or herself for caving in to the peer pressure. Samantha was obnoxious, but she should have never puffed on that joint. She knew better.

Oblivious to the young man who'd been watching the heated exchange and was now her shadow, Najee located then purchased the book she was looking for, before taking the escalator up to the second level. She ordered a skinny vanilla latte from the in-store Starbucks and grabbed a seat in the café next to the window.

The young man admired her wild, untamed hair and flawless honey-brown skin exposed by the barely-there tank top and jean shorts she was wearing. He sucked his teeth. Ray was going to have to let him do the honors of breaking this one in. As Najee removed the book from the cream-colored bag and opened it to the first page, the stranger removed his cell phone from his back pocket and texted.

I got a live one.

The phone immediately buzzed back. *Type?*

Exotic. Only top dollar for this one.

CHAPTER 23

Miles Day wandered around Children's Hospital feeling like he was trapped in a maze. He had been away from the hospital for a few weeks, and he was trying to melt back into the familiar flow. The morning was a blur. One patient after another made the time pass quickly, but he was fading fast. The lack of sleep was catching up to him.

Miles stopped at the nurses' station. The L-shaped hub buzzed with the sounds of an impending shift change as nurses greeted one another and exchanged patient reports. He glanced at the whiteboard. Dr. Sydney James was also in the building.

He leaned against the countertop and studied the clipboard with the printout of his active patients and the ones he'd seen and discharged. What was he going to say to her?

"Hey, Dr. Day." Jason, one of the few male nurses on staff, greeted him and interrupted his thoughts. "Good to have you back."

"Thanks, J." He smiled and returned to the printout in front of him. Throughout the day, he noticed the quick glances and hesitant stares from other staff, but he expected that.

The fallout from the fight at Lois the Pie Queen had tarnished his professional image. Last night, after arriving home, he opened a letter with a legal demand to pay ten thousand dollars for half the damages, and he didn't even blink. He was ashamed of the amount of damage they did to the small, family-friendly eatery. So, he wrote a check for the demand, added an additional two thousand dollars, and dropped it in the mail to the owner that morning. And since it was Donathan who initiated the physical contact with accusations of him sleeping with Sydney, he hoped his sorry ass had done the same.

Deciding he needed a jolt of caffeine, Miles made his way to the doctors' lounge and quickly brewed himself a cup of black tea. He took a seat on the leather couch and thumbed through the *Bay Area Medical Journal* as he waited for the liquid to cool enough for him to drink it. He tried to think about anything but Sydney, though he couldn't concentrate—too many things were going on in his head.

"Miles?"

He looked up into the face of Julia Stevens, the self-appointed queen bee of Children's Hospital Oakland. She was also the hospital busybody who had made it her job to stick her nose into everybody's business, including his.

"Julia." He smiled, picking up his cup of tea from the side table and taking a sip. "How are you?"

"I should be asking you that question, stranger." She leaned in and hugged Miles a little too long before taking the seat on the couch next to him. "It's so good to see you," she gushed, her long red hair brushing against his shoulder. Miles stayed quiet, staring at Julia, taking in her words. She continued.

"My schedule has been absolutely insane since you've been away. Not only did I cover those few extra shifts for you, but I'm also on the selection committee for the award you're reading about."

Miles raised an eyebrow, then looked down to the open pages of the magazine resting on his lap.

"The Dodson Society Award?"

"Yes, and we've selected a very worthy recipient this year. Dr. Maurice James, a distinguished cardiac surgeon at UCSF."

"James? Any relation to Sydney?"

"I guess you could say that. I mean there's no blood relation, but he's her father-in-law."

"Interesting. So, what's the award criteria?"

"The award is given annually to an outstanding member of the medical community in recognition of his or her contributions to research. Recipients are given a significant cash award, and an additional award is donated to their hospital in their honor."

"Sounds pretty cool."

"It's a very big deal in the Bay Area circles of who is who. And Sylver James, the wife of this year's recipient, is having a huge party to celebrate his achievement. All of the committee members were personally invited."

"Sounds like fun."

"Heeeey," she said, turning her body to face him. "Why don't you attend the party with me as my date? It'll be fun, and a great opportunity for you to rub elbows with the Bay Area elite."

Miles reached for an apple from the fruit bowl on the table in front of him and took a huge bite. "I don't know," he mumbled, talking with his mouth full. "I need to catch up on some things."

Julia stared at Miles a long moment, then she stood. "Don't tell me you're about to get mixed up with Sydney James again? Thought you learned your lesson with that one already," she said, her tone dripping with sarcasm.

"And what lesson would that be?"

"That she's a married woman, silly," she said, her demeanor quickly turning playful as she leaned in and squeezed his bicep. "And I, on the other hand, am not. Look, the party is in a few days, and it's a great opportunity for you to network. I'm sure those *other things* can wait."

Miles took another bite of the apple and chewed as he tossed around her proposition. His intuition told him this was a bad idea for two reasons, the first being he knew he had no business showing up at a private party for Donathan's father. And the second being he'd been hit on enough by women to see he was about to have a head-on collision with a Mack truck. Julia reminded him of his ex-wife, Stephanie, who created more than enough drama in his life. Julia was a beautiful woman, but her demeanor and attitude were a force that he would never in a million years want to tangle with romantically. Still, he couldn't pass up the opportunity to be introduced to the Bay Area's movers and shakers. As far as he was concerned, this wasn't a date. Just two colleagues attending a function together. He would worry about clarifying the boundaries of their friendship later.

"Alright, I'm in."

"Fantastic! The event is black tie, and I will have a car pick—"

"Whoa, no deal. I know you invited me, but how about I have a car pick you up? That's the least I can do."

"Of course," she said with a coy giggle.

CHAPTER 24

It was just past 2 a.m., and Donathan was wide awake, combing through printed newspaper articles of unsolved serial murder cases that fit Austyn's modus operandi. Glad he was home alone without Sydney hovering over his shoulder, he took a gulp from the mug of black coffee and replayed the Pleasanton surveillance video for the umpteenth time. He watched, then paused the tape at the same digital location, trying to catch a clear shot of the woman's face, but even without visual proof, he knew in his gut the image on the screen was Austyn Greene. The picture quality was grainy, but he watched the petite figure appear on the screen from out of the camera shot, then make her way toward the stairwell of the hotel, her head leaning toward the ground. The police hadn't seen this footage yet, but from what he saw on TV, they were acting way too conservative. If they continued on like this, they would never catch her.

As a psychologist, Donathan knew that to truly understand the depths of her depravity, he had to understand her unconscious mind, what made her tick. Until that happened, no one would be able to stop her.

He squeezed the bridge of his nose and all the while searched his mind for the whispers, the instincts on what to do next. His eyes grew heavy, and he reached for the coffee again but the cup was empty. He only had a few more hours to wrap this up and make his way to the bed before Sydney came home. The last thing he needed was for her to find him sitting at his desk again, and he had to make sure there were no visible signs of the video; otherwise, he'd have to explain how he came upon that little nugget.

Since his near-death experience at the hands of Austyn Greene, he hadn't returned to work. He didn't want his challenges to overflow to his patients, but he was due to start seeing patients again next week. His return to the radio station gig, on the other hand, was on hold indefinitely. When he met with the executives a few days before, they decided to take the wait-and-see approach. Initially, he thought with one less thing on his plate he could devote all his time to finding Austyn and getting his life back on track.

However, on his drive to Pleasanton, he noticed his likeness plastered on a few billboards along the I-80 corridor and felt a sense of urgency to get back in front of the mic again soon. He promised Sydney that he would let the police do their job, but the truth of the matter was, he couldn't fully concentrate on anything else until Austyn Greene was caught and behind bars receiving treatment.

With coffee in his cup, Donathan made his way back to his desk. He paused outside the home office and glanced toward the front door, then back toward the kitchen. He sniffed the air, thought he smelled something burning, but he quickly quelled the thought. Probably the coffee he had just brewed. He took a sip of the hot liquid and scalded his tongue.

"Dammit!" he groaned.

He didn't have time to linger. Sydney would be home soon. He made his way to the high-back leather chair and scooted closer to the desk. No need for sleeping pills tonight. His mind and body were exhausted and ready for sleep, but he needed a few more minutes.

His mind drifted to Payton. She'd been dealt a tough blow, confirming that Austyn Greene was her half sister. In the morning he would make it a point to call and check on her, and if she was receptive, he would refer her to a colleague to talk more about it. He copied the surveillance CD to his laptop, then removed a padded brown envelope from his desk drawer, packaged up the original, and addressed it to Detective Allen at the Pleasanton Police Department. Without a clear image of the woman's face, this wouldn't help their investigation much, but he didn't want to get in the way of justice.

He picked up one of the articles again and studied the tiny by-line. How did she murder all these people and not get caught? Her ability to go unnoticed was uncanny and another reason he had to watch his back. There were six dead in Los Angeles, and with the Pleasanton murder, three in the Bay Area. Was there a pattern here? If there was, he couldn't quite see it. Black men, Mexican men, city workers, and now a white man. Until now, these murders had faded into the background. He read that the six in Los Angeles were members of a street gang, and LAPD obviously hadn't put any resources into finding the killer: No one actually cared when a few street thugs ended up dead. Donathan sipped more coffee, but his eyelids grew heavier until he drifted off to sleep, facedown in the sea of articles strewn across his desk.

The shrill of the ringing telephone jarred Donathan awake. He was momentarily dazed, oblivious to the orange glow coming from the front window. He glanced at the wall clock, but before it could come into focus, the phone screamed again. He yanked up the handset.

"Hello."

"Baby, this is Mrs. Brown. I think that crazy gal don' come over here again. Come outside quick. Your front yard is on fire!"

CHAPTER 25

The soulful voice of Avery Sunshine blared through the car speakers as Payton coasted down the highway toward Pittsburg. She pressed the Call button on the steering wheel and instructed the automated voice to dial Sydney James. Three weeks had passed since they'd had a real girlfriend conversation, and they were long overdue. She'd purposely given her friend some breathing room to work on her marital issues, but three weeks was long enough.

She wondered how things were going between her and Donathan since her friend had returned home. "Hello?"

"Are you asleep?"

"I was taking a little nap."

"Girl, that's all you ever do. You're not pregnant, are you?"

"Sleep is needed when you work for a living, which is what I did last night. And no, I'm not pregnant."

"Is Donathan home?"

"No, he's not. He's helping his mother finalize a few things for his father's recognition dinner tonight."

"How did you get out of that one?"

"We had a grass fire in the compost bin last night, so I was designated to stay behind for the cleanup crew. Besides, there was no way I was going to volunteer for that. I love my mother-in-law dearly, but I can only take so much of her, especially now that her son has been plastered all over the front pages of the newspapers. They need to work through that privately."

Payton laughed. "Well, once I deal with my uncle, I was thinking about picking up some Mexican food and coming over."

"I'd like that."

"Alright, then I'll see you in a couple of hours."

She ended the call and continued to the Mar Ray Motel. She'd barely closed the door to her car when a young man in his mid-twenties approached her. His jeans were sagging, their waistband secured tightly around his hips with a belt and his T-shirt, emblazoned with the words "Head Nigga in Charge," was sagged across his yet-to-be-fully-developed chest.

Payton glanced at the cardboard box resting on her front seat and engaged her car alarm. She'd stopped at the real estate office in Concord to pick up the box before coming here, and even though she didn't believe there was anything valuable in the box, she didn't want to take any chances. She took a step back. "Have you ever heard of personal space?"

The scrawny man's wicked grin exposed a row of gold-capped front teeth. He took another step forward. "Yeah, I have. And that's exactly where you are . . . in Ray's personal space."

Payton stepped to the left, then to the right, but the man moved with her, his slender frame blocking her path.

"Look, I don't have time for your childish games, so if you'll excuse me." She forcefully moved past him. At Sheldon's door, she knocked and waited, but Sheldon didn't answer. She retrieved her cell phone from her sweat suit pocket and dialed his number. The phone rang a few times, then went to his voice mail.

"Damn."

Where the hell was he? It had been almost a week since she'd seen or heard from him. He'd never gone this long without contacting her. He hadn't responded to her text from yesterday, and that didn't make sense, especially since she had something he definitely wanted. Money.

The man laughed at her in a mocking tone as she walked back past him.

"He's not there."

"Tell me something I don't know," she mumbled, her steps measured and deliberate.

"What's it worth to you?"

Payton stopped mid-stride, then pivoted to face him. "What?"

He hitched up his sagging pants and hobbled toward her, the crotch resting at his knees. Payton shook her head. He'd be crippled by the time he was forty. She'd read an article the other day that noted sagging pants forced wearers to rotate their legs out in an awkward manner, and if done over time, could result in hip degeneration and lower back problems later in life.

"I said, what's it worth to you?"

"Look, Ray, or whatever your name is. Like I said before, I don't have time to play games."

"I don't play games." He stretched out his palm to her. "Money makes things work in Ray's personal space."

"Are you fucking serious?"

She shifted her weight from one foot to the other, taking in this pathetic, lost individual who was standing in front of her.

"You want the information or not?"

Payton sighed heavily as she reached into her jacket pocket and removed her small wallet. She took out a twenty-dollar bill and placed it in his outstretched hand.

He smirked. "Now, surely the information you want is worth more than a twenty."

"How much?" she demanded.

"For you . . . how about a Benjamin?"

Payton's eyes narrowed as she counted the remaining bills she had in her wallet and glimpsed the bright-white sneakers that adorned his feet. She couldn't believe she was getting shaken down by a damn tennis shoe pimp. She finished counting, then stared him in the eyes.

"I don't have a hundred dollars."

"That right there will be fine." He grinned.

She thrust the wad of money into his palm and watched as he neatly folded the bills in half and placed them in his front pocket.

"Try 4B. He's been spending a lot of time over there with that other uppity bitch," he spat out, then hobbled away and left Payton standing in the middle of the courtyard.

"Fucking predator," she mumbled as she followed him, making her way to the room next door where he had perched himself against the building. He propped one foot on the stucco. His eyes were glued to her when she reached the door and knocked quickly.

After a few seconds, the door jerked open, but only as far as the safety chain would allow.

"Who is it?" the female voice said, muffled from behind the rust-colored door.

Payton frowned, her eyes darting up and down the half-cracked door. She didn't know what she'd expected, but the twentysomething woman in front of her definitely wasn't it. The door obscured her face, and the mass of long golden braids further hid her features, but Payton could tell that she was young. Sheldon was old enough to be this girl's father.

"Can I help you?" the voice said, this time with more force.

"Is Sheldon here?"

"This isn't Sheldon's room."

"I know, but I got it on good authority that he hangs out here," Payton said, loud enough for Ray to hear. "Look, have you seen him or not?"

"Naw, he ain't here, and don't come to my damn room no more looking for him." The woman slammed the door shut.

Payton stepped back from the door like she'd been slapped. Why the hell was everybody so fucking rude? She turned and locked eyes with the figure who was still watching her. He smiled another toothy grin. *Ugh*, she thought and shook her head.

"What? Don't look at me like that," he teased.

Before she eased into her car, she turned around and took one last look at the now-closed door that had just been slammed in her face. The curtains moved, and an eerie feeling washed over her, making her breath catch in her throat. Something wasn't right. She could feel it.

Ray called out to her. "Who you gon' believe, me or that bitch?"

CHAPTER 26

The sound of a car horn rescued Najee from Tony's never-ending lecture. Before he could utter another word she grabbed her backpack and made a beeline for the front door.

"Don't forget what I told you," he boomed after her.

She couldn't believe the level of drama she had to put up with just to leave the freakin' house. Najee hurried down the sidewalk and just as she reached for the car door she gave a quick glance over her shoulder.

"Hey Lauren. I told Najee that I need to meet your parents. Can you set that up for me please?"

Lauren twisted her face, then quickly recovered. "Uh, sure thing, Mr. Barnes."

"Is there a problem Naj?" he questioned, almost as if daring her to show any sign of defiance so he could revoke his decision to let her get in the car driven by her sixteen-year-old friend.

"No problem," Naj replied coolly. He was embarrassing her in front of her friend—something their mother had never done.

"Thanks for coming with me," she said to Lauren as she buckled her seat belt and settled back against the leather.

"Are you sure going to meet this photographer guy is a good idea? And what planet is your brother from? I can't believe he wants to meet the parentals."

"Yes, I'm sure. Dante said it would take no more than thirty minutes tops and the pay is three hundred dollars."

"Cool. I told Sam we could all hang out after I pick my brother up from soccer camp."

Najee shifted in the passenger seat and faced her. "Lauren, I'm not trying to get in your business, but you need to be careful when it comes to Samantha. That girl is bad news."

"C'mon Naj, don't be so quick to judge. Sam is just—misunderstood."

"To you maybe. Ever wonder why she doesn't have any friends? And what's with the pot thing?"

"Cannabis is not a big deal. It's legal, it comes from the earth and I only need a few puffs to take the edge off. You're acting like I'm taking Ritalin or something."

"It's legal for adults, not a sixteen-year-old."

"Don't get all high and mighty on me now. I seem to recall you taking a few puffs yourself the other day."

"Something I've regretted since then," Najee replied with a dramatic sigh.

Ever since Lauren got her car it seemed as if everyone at school wanted to be her friend, and unfortunately she didn't have a discerning bone in her body.

Shirley Barnes had taught Najee early on that when it came to friends and acquaintances, she had to choose wisely. "People will want things from you because of what you can do for them," she'd warned her daughter.

"Don't say I didn't try to warn you."

The drive to Magnolia Street in the warehouse district of West Oakland went by quickly. As they cruised down the street, Najee read the text message on her phone then carefully perused the buildings for the address the photographer had given her.

"This street looks so deserted," Lauren commented.

"I'm sure it's fine. He said once we got here to buzz the suite."

They arrived at the front of the building numbered 212 and scrolled the roster for Suite L-B. A man's voice and the loud clicking of the door lock release startled them both.

"C'mon up the stairs and make a left at the end of the hallway."

"Dante?" Najee questioned.

"In the flesh."

On the way up the stairs, nerves started to get the best of Najee. She had never modeled before and wasn't sure what to expect. When Dante texted to offer the quick modeling gig the first thing that had come to mind was having her own money. Since she wasn't sixteen yet, she wasn't old enough for a summer job, and having her own money would make her feel like less of a burden to her brother. She pulled at her tank top, feeling self-conscious about her attire.

"Stop fidgeting," Lauren hissed. "You look fine."

The door to the suite was flung open and they were welcomed into the space by a familiar thirty-something man wearing jeans, a black t-shirt, and multiple gold chains.

"Najee, you didn't tell me you were bringing a friend." He reached forward, extended his hand, and pulled her into him, almost knocking her off balance. "I'm Dante."

"Lauren."

"Would you girls like something to drink? Water, soda pop, wine coolers?"

"A wine—"

"Water. We will both have water," Najee responded, giving Lauren a stern side-eye. Sneaking wine coolers out of her parent's fridge was one thing but this was entirely another.

"You can get changed in there, he said, pointing to one of only two doors in the huge space. Lauren can stay out here and keep me company."

With only a leather couch and a few box lights in the far corner of the loft, the room was sparse, nothing like the type of photography studio she'd imagined.

Najee entered the dressing room, closed and locked the door behind her. She was overcome with feelings of deep apprehension when her eyes landed on a fuchsia two-piece string bikini that left little to the imagination. Of course she'd seen the ads with Victoria's Secret models clad in next to nothing but there was no way she was putting this on. If this was what she was supposed to model, then she would have to pass.

Bikini in hand, she opened the door and made her way across the room to where Dante worked to adjust and position the lights.

"Excuse me, but I can't wear this."

Dante looked at the swimsuit then back at Najee, smirking lust-fully. "That outfit is for the next model. Your attire is the workout gear hanging on the rack. You're not ready for that one yet."

Najee's face flushed beet red before she turned away and hurried back to the dressing room. She changed into the workout gear, swiped clear gloss across her lips and fluffed her natural curls. She was embarrassed and wanted to get this shoot over with.

Thirty minutes later, Dante counted as he placed the crisp hundred-dollar bills into the palm of Najee's hand. "One hundred, two hundred, three hundred. You're a natural."

"Thanks," Najee squealed. Cash in hand made the hot blinding lights worth her while. At first, her stomach had been in knots, but then Dante turned on Lizzo and directed her every move, which made the time in front of the camera pass quickly. She was in utter disbelief when he said they were done.

"So, do you think you can do jobs like this for me again? I'll have more gigs just like this one real soon.

"Yes."

"Alright, I'll be in touch."

Dante watched from the window as Lauren and Najee climbed into the brand-new Honda Civic and pulled away from the curb. He had expected the exotic beauty to come alone and the friend showing up threw a monkey wrench in his plan. He reached in his pocket, retrieved his cell, and dialed the familiar number.

"Speak on it."

"She brought a friend, so no go today."

"Why not two for one?"

"It crossed my mind, but the friend would bring heat we want no part of. I was right about the mark. Her mother is dead, so she probably lives in some type of group home—the kind of situation that's good for our business."

"How long? I already promised this one to Atlanta."

"She's going to need to be broke in—"

"Good. New pussy is the best pussy."

"Man, I hear you, and when the time is right, I'll bring her to you."

CHAPTER 27

Sydney was enjoying her afternoon of solitude, but it also gave her room to think. Her relationship with Donathan was a disaster. She missed the easiness of it, and now they were out of sync. Things were so tense that she was looking forward to some time by herself, but she was also coveting some time alone with her friend.

Even though Payton wasn't the most sympathetic person, they had a lot of catching up to do. She clicked on the seventy-inch TV, which took up a good portion of the family room wall, then turned to the news. The banner ticking across the lower screen read *Breaking News*, and on the screen a red pickup truck with lawn equipment in the truck's bed caught her attention.

She blinked a few times in confusion. It looked almost identical to the way she'd seen it when he rear-ended her a few weeks ago, except the front windshield was shattered with a few bullet holes on the driver's side. She turned up the volume so she could hear the female reporter.

"The Oakland Police Department had an overnight standoff with a man on Twenty-Third and Bancroft. Police say the man tried to run them over with his vehicle, and fearing for their safety, shots were fired. The driver has been confirmed dead, but no information about his identity has been released until notification of his next of kin. Stay with KTVU2 News for more on this developing story."

Sydney stared at the television bewildered. *Damn.* Was that the same guy she had the accident with? The man was crazy, true enough, but he needed mental health services, not a bullet to the head. This was the fifth officer-involved shooting of an unarmed man in the United States in less than a week. These killings had to stop.

When the security gate chimed, Sydney hopped off the couch, made her way to the wall display, and let Payton in through the front gates. She padded barefoot to the front door, opened it, and stood in the doorway, waiting for the Lexus to come to a stop.

Payton exited the car and made her way toward Sydney, balancing bags of takeout food on top of a banker's box. When she reached her, Sydney grabbed the food.

"I thought you said the fire was in the compost bin? Your entire front yard is torched. What the hell happened?" Payton asked, stepping inside the foyer and using her hip to close the front door behind them.

"According to the El Cerrito Fire Department, the mixing of old and new grass clippings in our compost bin got too hot and caused spontaneous combustion."

"Spontaneous who?"

"My thoughts exactly, but what it boils down to is that the grass in the compost bin had some kind of chemical reaction and ignited all by itself last night."

"That shit sounds crazy."

"I know. It happened around four this morning. If it weren't for Mrs. Brown, the house might have caught on fire."

"I swear, that woman doesn't miss a beat. Her nosy ass just waved at me as I was driving through the gate."

"For once, I'm grateful for nosy and that damn purple sweet potato pie she makes."

They both laughed.

Sydney grabbed two plates from the cabinet, along with some

silverware. She then took two stemmed glasses from the wine rack and retrieved the chilled bottle of V. Sattui Gamay Rouge from the fridge, filling their glasses.

"So, what's in the box?"

"Once we eat, that's what we're about to find out."

An empty plate and a bottle and a half of wine later, they sat cross-legged on the floor with their backs resting against the sofa, the banker's box between them.

Payton removed the lid and scanned the contents. Her hand went to the groupings of pictures held together by rubber bands. She pulled out a few stacks, keeping one for herself and handing the other to Sydney.

They continued drinking wine and laughing at the many pictures of Payton growing up. Sydney joked about the various hair ribbons in the photos, laughed at the outrageous bangs, and scanned the familiar faces of Payton's grandparents, father, and uncles during happier times. They had gone through most of the box's contents when Sydney picked up a yellowing envelope at the bottom.

The letter was addressed to Payton. The sender was listed as Lois Greene. The postmark date had faded, but the envelope was mailed from Los Angeles, California. Sydney opened the letter, and a picture of a woman holding a baby fluttered into her lap. She began reading.

Dear Payton,

Where do I begin? Mommy has been clean and sober for twelve months. I know I have caused you pain, but Mama was sick, baby. I'm coming back to Pittsburg for you, and I'm going to move you to Los Angeles with me and your new sister. Her name is Austyn, and she looks just like you did when you were a baby. I can't wait for you to meet her. When you get this letter, give me a call at 323-555-5678. I know I left you behind, but I'm coming back to get you. I promise.

Love,

Lois

Sydney was stunned. Her eyes narrowed as she read the yellowing paper again, but the words on the page stayed the same. She picked up the picture from her lap and studied the woman and the child.

"I don't look that bad," Payton said, yanking the picture from Sydney's grasp.

She thrust the letter in Payton's direction and watched her as she read. This didn't make sense. The woman who'd tried to kill Donathan and her was Payton's sister? The woman Donathan was so desperate to find was her best friend's mother? Sydney's mind raced like an old still movie trying to fill in the gaps. She and Payton had been friends since they met at UCLA, and she knew Payton's mother had abandoned her, but that topic of conversation had always been off-limits.

When Payton spoke of her family and childhood, it was always about her grandparents and her father. But she never spoke her mother's name. This news was going to devastate her best friend, and she was glad she'd be able to support her through it. She stared at Payton, waiting for the emotions to bubble to the surface, but after several minutes, the reaction she expected never came.

"Well, I'll be damned," Sydney said. "I can't believe you knew this and didn't say a word!"

"Sydney, please don't get upset. When I found out Austyn shared the same last name as my mother, I thought it was purely a coincidence, but after running into Donathan yesterday in Pleasanton, he confirmed for me what I had begun to suspect."

"This is un-fucking-believable! Donathan James? My husband? And neither of you thought you should tell me?" Sydney rose to her feet, knocking over the almost-empty glass of wine that rested beside her. "You two are a piece of work!" She made her way toward the kitchen, Payton close on her heels.

"C'mon, Syd, it's not like that. My suspicions weren't confirmed until yesterday. But this picture puts the nail in the coffin. Austyn Greene really is my half sister."

Sydney stepped around her friend, making her way back toward the stain on the carpet with a towel and a canister of salt in hand. She kneeled down, covered the red spot with the white crystals, and waited until they turned pink.

"Well, say something."

"What do you want me to say?" Sydney snapped, her eyes sharp as daggers. "That my best friend doesn't trust me enough to share what's going on in her life? Or that my husband is a goddamn hypocrite? What exactly do you want me to say?"

Before Payton could respond, the sound of the front door opening and closing distracted her. A knot in her stomach tightened when she saw Tony and Donathan appear in the doorway. Tony dipped his head, avoiding eye contact with her, and Donathan looked busted. No words passed between the couples for what seemed like an eternity. Then Sydney sprang up from the floor and headed for the stairs.

"Baby, wait," Donathan pleaded, following after her.

Tony closed the distance and gently caught Payton by the elbow. "C'mon, let's give them some privacy," he said and led her toward the kitchen. An aroused shiver trickled down the length of her spine.

"Get your hands off me," she said, her dark brown eyes squinting to almost slits as she came face-to-face with the man who had not returned a single one of her text messages or phone calls in the past few weeks.

Once in the kitchen, he leaned against the granite countertop and stared at her, his face void of emotion. And just like that her nipples stiffened under the sheer blue blouse. What the hell was wrong with her? She searched his eyes, wondered if he had even thought about her, and if he did, why did she feel so fucking lonely standing less than six feet away from him? She folded her arms across her chest, then looked away.

"Look," he cajoled. "My life is—"

"You couldn't return a text message?" Payton interrupted. "One minute you're in my bed, and the next it was like you dropped off the face of the earth. No call, no text—"

"My mother was fucking dying! What don't you get about

that? And on the worst day of my life, I had to walk past a window seeing the woman I-I- with some dude's hand in her mouth. So, excuse me if I'm not behaving how you want me to," he said, his voice trailing off.

"I thought we had an understanding."

"So, help me understand the parameters of the 'understanding'," he said, using air quotes.

Payton stood speechless, pushing back tears as she was confronted by her lover, a man who had promised her nothing but gave her everything. She digested why Tony was upset with her and had come to the conclusion that even though their relationship wasn't defined, she, too, would have been furious if she saw him being hand-fed by some random bitch.

"That shit you pulled was pretty fucked up," he said, interrupting her thoughts. "I've replayed it over and over again, and my conclusion is still the same. Your ass is spoiled and selfish, and you always want shit when you want it. All you had to say was you were no longer feeling our arrangement, and that would have been enough."

Tony crossed the room and took a seat on one of the leather bar stools. Payton followed.

"Tony, please," she murmured.

"Please what, Payton?" he asked coldly.

His words hung between them like a block of ice. What did she want from him? A monogamous relationship? She blinked rapidly at the thought.

Stroking his arm, she carefully eased her body between his legs, but right now she was spiraling into an unfamiliar abyss. She kissed him on his jawline, traced her tongue around his earlobe, and nuzzled the crook of his neck.

"I don't know how to do this…" she murmured, feeling the pressure of his growing erection. Payton lifted her head and searched his face for clues.

"Payton, now is not the time for this."

"Why not?" she said, sighing heavily and moving in closer, this time stealing a kiss on his lips. She could feel him growing harder against her thigh, and her hand swooped down to massage the bulge she was so fond of. His mouth was saying one thing, but his growing manhood was telling her what he wanted. He studied her a long moment, then kissed her roughly, taking control of the situation.

Payton shivered as his tongue owned her mouth before trailing down the column of her throat, while his hands skimmed her spine, finally cupping her ass and pulling her closer to him. Payton moaned, breathless, arching her back and pushing her breasts into his face.

He kissed her again, long and hard, and she kissed him back. When they came up for air, his eyes locked with hers, and his brooding stare cut through her like a newly sharpened knife. She held her breath, feeling exposed and naked. Tony stood, adjusted his jeans, and tried to take a step back, but Payton wrapped her hand in the hem of his shirt to keep him close. At first, he looked uncomfortable, like he was fighting a war within himself, then he stared at her for what seemed like an eternity before he spoke.

"C'mon. We have some unfinished business to take care of."

CHAPTER 28

Sheldon Jones quietly dragged his bike through the deserted courtyard of the Mar Ray Motel. He thought about chaining it to the pipe outside his room, but worried that might make too much noise and decided against it. He searched for any movement of the curtains as he eased by her room, then it dawned on him that he knew nothing about this woman, including her name. Who the hell was she? And why was she so interested in Payton and Lois?

By the time he reached his door, he glanced over his shoulder one last time and noticed a hooded silhouette across the courtyard, standing in the shadows.

"Hey, I need to talk to you."

Sheldon turned away in a panic, jiggling the key in the lock, knocking his bike over in the process. The door opened, but he wasn't fast enough to scramble inside his room before she placed a hand on his shoulder.

"If I didn't know any better, I'd say you were avoiding me." She eyed him suspiciously and hovered close as he bent down to pick up his bike. When he stood back up, she gestured toward his open door, a clear baggie pinched between her fingers.

"Where are your manners? Aren't you going to invite me inside?"

Visibly agitated, Sheldon rolled his bike inside the room and propped it next to the window. She was the reason he hadn't been back to his room in two days. The light from his cell phone screen sitting on the table caught his attention. He reached to pick it up, but the woman yanked the cord, sending the phone flying off the table.

"What the hell do you think you're doing?" Sheldon yelled, reaching for her as she backed away from him. "Give me that."

"I'll give you the damn phone back, but first I want to know why your niece came to my room looking for you today."

"I don't know who the hell you are, but you need to get the hell out of my room!"

She reached into her pocket, pulled out another white baggie, and brandished both of them in his face. "Do you still want me to go?"

Sheldon froze, his eyes never leaving the tiny packages of crack cocaine. He hadn't gotten high in a few days, and he needed to feel that euphoric rush with imaginary particles floating in front of his face. He had no idea what this girl was up to, but he could feel it in his bones that it wasn't right. Even if she was feeding him his next high, he didn't have to tell her much. Just enough for her to give him what he wanted and leave. "What do you want?" he begged, his voice trembling with desperation.

"That's better. Now, I'm going to ask my question again. Are you listening?"

Sheldon nodded, and his body went numb. His stress level was so high he thought he'd drown in it. He couldn't concentrate on anything but how it would feel to inhale the thick white smoke into his lungs. But first, he had to convince her to give him the drugs. If that failed, he could overpower her and just take them. A trickle of snot ran from his nose, and he swiped it with the sleeve of his sweatshirt.

"Why did your niece come to my room looking for you today?"

"Payton was here?"

"Don't try to play me, old man. If you don't start talking, I'm leaving and taking my baggies with me—"

"I don't know why she would come to your room. I haven't seen or talked to her since she brought me here."

"What did you tell her about me?"

"Nothing," he said, his eyes darting from the plastic baggies to his phone, which she was holding in her right hand. "I can't talk to her without a phone."

"You better not be lying to me."

"I swear," he pleaded.

Sheldon glared at her, growing more impatient by the minute. He didn't want to answer any more of her goddamn questions. He wanted to get high.

She tossed the phone in his direction. "Check your voice mail messages."

"Why?"

"Just do it!"

He placed the phone to his ear and listened.

"There's only one message," he lied. There was only one voice message, but after typing in his password, he saw a text message from Payton that read: *I'm on my way to Pittsburg. Be in your room. It's important.*

"Put the call on speaker," she demanded.

Sheldon reluctantly did as he was told. The voice message had to be from Payton, too, because she was the only one who had the number. He held his breath and waited for Payton's voice to amplify into the room.

"Uncle Sheldon, I haven't heard from you in a few days. I need to talk to you. Call me back."

His eyes drifted away for a moment, contemplating his next move. He wondered if the woman had more than the two packets in her pocket. Wondered what it would feel like to lock himself in the bathroom and take that first hit. She tossed two baggies in his direction and made her way to the door.

"Pace yourself. The last thing I need for you to do is have a heart attack," she said, closing the door behind her. Sheldon jumped up, locked the door, and engaged the safety chain. Then, leaning against the door, he slid helplessly down to the floor. He wondered what was so important, but his mind wouldn't stay focused on Payton. Instead, he drifted back to that woman who'd just left his room. That fake blond bitch was trouble, but there was nothing he could do about it now. He reached for one of the baggies she'd tossed at him, retrieved the lighter and pipe from his pocket, and prepared to take a trip that would make him forget about everything.

CHAPTER 29

Najee lay in bed, too revved up to fall back to sleep. She'd been awake for hours thinking about Blue's pool party and couldn't wait to see her real friends, sans Samantha. She'd been looking forward to this event for the last few days, but the fact that she'd barely spoken to her best friend in almost a week was cause for anxiety. And since they were not on speaking terms, Najee knew it would be awkward spending the night at Lauren's place, so she opted to stay at her friend Nicole's instead. She missed Lauren, but when she saw her in person today she was going to make it clear to her that as long as she was smoking pot and hanging out with a loser like Samantha, they had nothing to talk about.

Najee showered, got dressed, then packed her backpack with the things she needed for the sleepover. She came across a card from Dante. She had to admit that when he approached her in the café, told her he was looking for models and had the perfect job for her right away it was almost unbelievable. She remembered him saying she could make lots of cash, and now that she'd done one gig, she wanted to do more so she could buy herself a car. Her excitement dissipated. There was no way Tony would let her model or do anything else. At first, she thought the permission slip with a guardian's signature would be a barrier for her, but Dante took the consent with her Aunt Rosemary's name forged on it and didn't even look at it twice. She was still mortified that she just blurted out to a perfect stranger that her mother was dead. But her epiphany didn't seem to faze the man at all. In fact, he assured her he had lots of girls with her exact same situation and they could work something out.

Najee tossed the card into the wastebasket and fell back onto the bed. Enough of those thoughts... Her cell phone began to ring. She looked down at the phone lying next to her. Her brother's name flashed across the display screen. She thought about sending him to voice mail, but she decided against it and answered on the fourth ring.

"Hello."

"Hey, kid. What's up?"

"Nothing. Getting ready to leave for the party."

"Sorry, I ran a little over helping Donathan and can't drop you off at the party like we planned. Is your friend Lauren picking you up? I still need to meet her parents."

Najee fell silent. He was sorry, but she was elated. When he called earlier asking if she could get a ride because something came up, she'd been trying to figure out how to tell Tony that her plans had changed. Since the blowup with Lauren on Bay Street, she was no longer sleeping over at Lauren's house, choosing to bunk with her friend Nicole instead. But if she told Tony the truth, he'd have lots of questions she didn't feel like answering right now. Anyway, what was the harm? He'd met both Lauren and Nicole before, but he hadn't met Nicole's parents either. "Najee?" he said, interrupting her thoughts.

"I'm waiting for my ride now."

"Okay. Can you do me a favor?"

"What's that?"

"Can you check in with me before you go to bed tonight?"

"What? C'mon, Tony," she whined. "I'm not a baby."

"Okay. Okay. Did you feed the kitten?"

"Yes, all done. I left enough food for her until I get home tomorrow."

"Alright, but promise me, if you need me, no matter what time it is, you will call me."

"I'm sure I'll be fine, but okay, I promise."

After what seemed like never-ending prying, rescue came in the form of a ping from her cell phone alerting her the ride-share service had arrived. She knelt down to pet the kitten.

"Make sure you use the litter box," she cooed, brushing the tiny feline's multicolored coat.

She slung her backpack over one shoulder, then surveyed her image one last time in the full-length mirror, making sure she was ready for the summer party of the year. She wore cutoff denim shorts over a yellow two-piece swimsuit, a fitted orange T-shirt with *I Got Sunshine* emblazoned across the front, and blinged-out Converse Chuck Taylor All-Stars. She liked the way her sun-kissed ringlets framed her face. Before setting the alarm, she peeked out the foyer blinds to see the car waiting with the recognizable decal affixed to the window. A young black guy who reminded her of Snoop Dogg smiled at her as she slid into the back seat of the vehicle. Glued to her cell phone, Najee rode in silence as they coasted down the street.

When they reached the stop sign at the bottom of the hill, the car paused for longer than the usual three-count beat. Najee didn't pay it too much attention at first, then suddenly, the clicking sound of the door locks disengaged and both back doors jerked open at once. A black and Hispanic man jumped into the back seat on either side of her. They sandwiched Najee close, muscular thighs pressing hard against her legs. Startled screams reverberated through the car as Najee felt a stranger's hand clamp over her arm. She tried to snatch her arm back, but his grip was too tight. She took a second look at the black man. He looked familiar, but before she could put two and two together, the Hispanic man grabbed her elbow. "Stop it! Get your hands off me!" she yelled, her arms and legs flailing helplessly.

"What the hell!" the driver barked.

Najee tried to move. She couldn't. Her wild eyes darted left, then right. "Let me go!" she pleaded. Her eyes fixated on the young black man, before they began blinking rapidly at the familiarity of his face.

Bile tickled her throat, but she swallowed, panting for breath as the man she recognized as the photographer from Bay Street covered her mouth and nose with an old dingy rag that reeked of rotten eggs. She thrashed her head from side to side, sucked and swallowed air greedily, and felt herself suffocating.

The Snoop Dogg lookalike watched the scene unfold through the rearview mirror. He scrutinized the young girl's breaths as they went from quick and shallow to slow and deep, and then her body went limp.

"Dante, what the hell is going on? This girl is not like the usual ones. I should have known something was up when you had me camping out in this neighborhood for the last few days. I'm not going to jail for no damn kidnapping charge. Does Ray—?"

"Man, just shut the fuck up and drive!"

CHAPTER 30

Pican's was nestled in the thriving Uptown District of downtown Oakland. As the limo waited to pull up to the curb, Sydney fidgeted in the back seat, eager to escape Donathan's piercing stares. She'd had enough of him trying to convince her of his truth, which as far as she was concerned, was a flat-out lie. But her emotions were conflicted. One minute she was hysterical about being lied to. And the next she felt like a hypocrite, knowing she had secrets of her own. It made no sense to her why Donathan and Payton both felt the need to keep her in the dark about Austyn being Payton's half sister. Why did the people who claimed to love her feel the need to pick and choose what information they felt was relevant for her to know? Did they think she was so fragile that she would break at the first sign of pressure? She was a doctor, for Christ's sake, and she successfully dealt with crisis situations daily. The fact that this little tidbit of information directly affected her life gave her the right to know.

Avoiding his eye contact, she stared out the window at the sea of expensive cars waiting to be valet parked and was grateful she hadn't driven her own vehicle. She'd tried, but Donathan wouldn't go for that. His stance was that they arrive together or not attend at all. Sydney knew it would devastate her father-in-law if his only son were a no-show, and it would also give his mother's socialite circle something else to talk about. Dr. Maurice James deserved nothing but accolades for his hard work and dedication to the field of medicine, and she refused to be the reason for disappointment to a man who deserved nothing but praise. Maybe his wayward son could take a page or two out of his book.

When Sydney and Donathan stepped inside the trendy restaurant, people were trickling in. The dramatic Southern décor evoked the feel of sophistication, a prime establishment for upscale entertaining. Sylver James, her mother-in-law, had hired D.R. Roberts Event Management, and they'd further transformed the place to look like something out of a designer magazine. Jazz music, elaborate floral arrangements, handwritten place cards, and chairs draped in royal purple satin, with expertly tied chocolate-brown bows, were first-class touches. "Donathan James! Is that you?"

A man resembling a heavyset George Jefferson approached them and embraced Donathan in a bear hug, then stepped back to give him a once-over.

"Man, the older you get, the more you look like Maurice. And who is this lovely lady here?"

"Dr. Alfred, this is my wife, Dr. Sydney James."

Sydney extended her hand, but was quickly pulled into a friendly embrace. "No handshakes here, we're family."

"Nice to meet you, Dr. Alfred."

Donathan raised an eyebrow and smiled. "Dr. Alfred, if I didn't know any better, I'd say you're getting fresh with my wife." He placed his hand in the small of Sydney's back, and she wanted to swat it away. Instead she saw this as an opportunity to excuse herself.

"I'll be right back." They were barely on speaking terms, but she would do her best this evening to leave the drama at home. But she couldn't help being angry and afraid. The root of everything wrong in their life right now was because Donathan had failed to tell her about the deranged woman who had drugged and stalked him. She looked down at her hand. To the naked eye, the scar was completely healed, but his lies had almost cost her the ability to perform surgery. Austyn Greene had proven she was a fucking nutcase, and all things related to her whereabouts should be handled by the police. Not by Donathan and Payton.

In the powder room, Sydney realized she was alone and audibly sighed once the door closed behind her. She surveyed her image in the full-length mirror, and did a half turn to admire how she looked from behind. The diamond choker sparkling around her neck accentuated the plunging neckline in the front and back of her long, fitted black dress. Her hair was pulled back into a tight chignon, and her makeup was minimal and flawless.

She retrieved her lipstick from her black-jeweled clutch and reapplied it to perfection. As she smoothed the fabric of her dress down her hips, the door opened, and Julia Stevens sashayed in.

Although Julia usually wore her hair straight and sleek, tonight her bright red tress was fluffed around her shoulders and teased out like a banshee. She'd opted for an above-the-knee cocktail dress that Sydney thought made her look cheap. A few years older than both Sydney and Miles, Julia's garb seemed to be screaming, *I want to look younger.* And if that's what Julia wanted, she had failed miserably. The two women stared at one another in silence before Sydney finally looked away.

"You look stunning," Julia said, the words seeming to fall out of her mouth before she could catch them.

"Thanks," Sydney mumbled.

Before Miles, these two weren't the best of friends. Nevertheless, they had been cordial and could move around in the same space without killing each other. But ever since Sydney returned to work, it seemed like Julia was on a mission to make Sydney's hospital existence a living hell.

"Excuse me," Sydney said, brushing past her and reaching for the door.

"You better stay glued to the hubby tonight. We don't want a repeat of that barbaric behavior from that horrid little diner."

"Julia, my husband is not in the habit of having confrontations with men."

"Maybe not, but he is intrigued by one man in particular," she said, her voice elevating then trailing off.

Sydney stopped short; she wasn't in the mood for Julia's antics tonight.

"Is Miles here?"

"Yes," Julia purred. "He's my date this evening."

A warning voice in Sydney's head sounded. *Oh, shit.* She had purposely been avoiding Miles, and for once, Julia was right. The last thing she needed was for him and Donathan to be in close proximity. Especially since Donathan had threatened to confront Miles again.

"Excuse me."

Sydney emerged from the ladies' room, her strides measured and confined by the seams of her evening gown. She maneuvered her way through the expertly placed tables like a woman on a mission. Everything seemed louder than before. The clatter coming from the kitchen and the hum of people socializing seemed to be elevated a few decibels. Before she could locate Donathan, she practically bumped into Miles, who was reaching for a glass of champagne from one of the passing servers.

"Well, this is a surprise," she quipped, admiring the tailored fit of his tuxedo, then inwardly chastising herself for noticing. The crisp white shirt contrasted nicely with his milk-chocolate skin, and his dreads were pulled back off his face, the tips resting in a bundle between his shoulder blades. Miles oozed sexiness, and any woman in her right mind would appreciate what she was seeing. He threw her an appreciative smile, and if she didn't know better, she would have sworn his dimples winked at her. His dark eyes were mesmerizing.

She nervously glanced over her shoulder. "I had no idea you were going to be here tonight."

"Well, Julia invited me as her guest, and I thought it would be a great opportunity to network and meet new people. I mean, I've never had the pleasure of meeting the guest of honor, but I've heard wonderful things about him, and I'm looking forward to it."

He stared at her, his eyes seeming to bury themselves deep into her core. Since his return from Chicago, something about him had changed.

"Well, I might be a little biased, but my father-in-law is very deserving of the honor and definitely someone you should meet," she said, managing to keep her cool. She stole another quick glance over her shoulder.

"What's the matter? Is your husband suddenly going to appear and start another fight with me because we're talking?" he said, his smile a little sinister this time.

Suddenly, she felt a strange pull in the pit of her stomach. Her mind told her to excuse herself and go find Donathan, but her feet wouldn't move. She stood paralyzed as Miles raked his eyes over the length of her body, and she blinked, trying to banish the soft flutters rolling around in her stomach. His lips curved into a seductive grin, and he leaned in close, the hairs of his neatly trimmed goatee brushing her earlobe.

"I know what you're thinking," he whispered.

The rush of cool air where his warm breath had been caused Sydney to shiver. Her cheeks grew warm as she thought about how she'd used Miles to numb the pain of her troubled marriage. What had started out as an innocent lunch between friends had ended with her having too much to drink and initiating sexual contact. The *old* Miles had been the perfect gentleman, if you consider the fact that after he made her come with his mouth, he'd had enough sense to stop the encounter. But this *new* Miles would have sealed the deal. Her nipples beaded, and she crossed her arms over her chest to hide them pressing against the sheer fabric of her dress.

A flash of red silk in her peripheral view caught Sydney's attention. Her eyes narrowed as she watched Julia, her lips pursed tightly into a frown, storm in their direction. Sydney had forgotten all about this miserable bitch. Here she had been worried about Donathan making a scene and hadn't taken into account Julia. Miles followed her gaze.

"We have some unfinished business, and you need to stop running from me," he said, turning on his heels to intercept an irate Julia and usher her back toward the ladies' room.

For a moment, Sydney stood still, allowing his words to penetrate. What the hell was she doing? Had she lost her damn mind? When she turned toward the backlit bar, all the air left her at once.

Perched on the corner of the massive mahogany counter, Donathan raised his glass tumbler of dark liquid in a mock toast and tilted his head in her direction before gulping the full contents. Sydney's body stiffened as the bartender immediately poured him another and he tossed back the second drink. What the hell was he doing? Hard liquor always made him sick. He drank a glass of wine every now and again, but this was totally out of character. She closed the distance between them and arrived just as he was about to turn up the third glass.

"What are you doing?" she hissed, noticing many more people had filtered into the now-filled room.

"You didn't seem too worried about what I was doing a few seconds ago," he spat, then turned up the amber liquid.

"What are you talking about?" she questioned, hoping the guilt she was feeling wasn't plastered all over her face.

"Did you invite him here?"

"No, I didn't."

Donathan motioned for the bartender again, but Sydney quickly pried the glass from his hand and shook her head at the man approaching with a bottle.

"You know I'm about two seconds from knocking that arrogant bastard on his ass."

"This is not the time or place for that," she spat, grateful he had enough sense to keep his voice down.

"I know you fucked him, Sydney. Admit it!"

"Ladies and gentlemen, let's put our hands together and welcome Dr. and Mrs. Malcolm Tulane James."

People quickly lined up on both sides of the aisle for the much-anticipated grand entrance. Sylver and Dr. Malcolm James breezed down the elaborate purple carpet, a copycat of the popular Hollywood trend. Grateful for the distraction, Sydney gleamed at her in-laws then back at her husband, who was now standing ramrod-straight. If he did have any type of alcohol-induced buzz, it appeared to have instantaneously dissipated. Silence hung between them. Lately, every time Donathan accused her of fucking Mile, her confession bubbled closer to the surface, ready to spring from her mouth involuntarily. Her conscience told her that was the right thing to do, but the consequences would be the end of her marriage. Besides, there had been a few times when rumors were flying around about Donathan's indiscretions, and although she never had any physical proof, he hadn't been so quick to confess his sins either. For his sake and her own, she needed to put his suspicions to rest once and for all. Sydney glanced over her shoulder and locked eyes with Miles, whose heated stares seemed to be caressing her bare back. He winked, and she could see his brain working behind those dark brown eyes. Her own mind immediately went into overdrive, and she had an epiphany. With the disdain Donathan had for Miles, the plan was a little risky. But if Miles did exactly as she asked him to, her marriage might live to see another day. Now all she had to do was ask him.

CHAPTER 31

Hunched down in the driver's seat of the blue Toyota with the camera resting on his lap, Holsey sat across the street from Glover House, hoping to catch a glimpse of his mark. He didn't have to wait long. A hooded silhouette exited the side gate that led to the backyard. From the shape and size, he presumed it was a woman. She looked to be about five foot seven, no more than 130 pounds. She was wearing dark jeans and the dark hoodie, and she held a small mag flashlight in her hand. He reached for his camera, angled, and focused the infrared zoom lens.

"Well, I'll be damned." He chuckled to himself.

He clicked off a few quick shots. It didn't get any better than this. He was hired to find Lois Greene, but Austyn Greene was the collateral. If he had a hand at capturing the Bay Area's most wanted woman, his face would be on all the news outlets, and that would be good for business. He'd also be eligible to collect the reward. He sent a quick text, waited for the response, then sent another one.

Every cop in the Bay Area was looking for this girl, and here she was, hiding in plain sight. He put down the camera and lit up a cigarette, taking a long drag before dumping the ashes in the overflowing ashtray.

He watched Austyn go from window to window, but when a

neighbor's motion detector floodlights came on, she scurried away. When he zoomed in, he saw her getting into some old clunker. He zoomed in more, onto her license plate, and clicked.

The dim headlights flickered on, and the car pulled off from the curb without hesitation. Not wanting to take the chance of being seen, Holsey waited a beat before he made a U-turn and followed. She'd made it to the end of the block, but he wouldn't have any trouble keeping up, since the busted taillight on the car was like following a trail of bread crumbs. After driving a few miles, she made a left turn onto the main drag. Holsey stayed a few car lengths back, taking extra care not to be seen, but he wasn't really worried that an old white guy would register on her radar.

Once they crossed over Highway 4, she turned into a cheap little motel tucked next to a fire station. He grinned at the nerve of this girl. No one would ever be looking for her here. He eased past the driveway, made a quick U-turn at the traffic light, and pulled into a deserted parking lot across the street. He dimmed his headlights and parked out of sight, but he kept the engine running. He was getting too old to be crouched down in cars and running all-night surveillance. In his mind, there were two options for his next move. He could turn what he learned over to Donathan for a few extra bucks or toss it into the lap of the Oakland Police Department. Weighing his options, he eyed the seedy motel across the street where he'd just seen Austyn use a key to enter a room.

With that thought, Holsey took a long drag from his newly lit cigarette, turned on his headlights, and headed toward the freeway to sleep on it. Come daybreak he knew exactly where to find her.

CHAPTER 32

When Austyn opened the door to her room, she was startled to find Ray, the self-appointed motel pimp, perched on her bed. She hesitated briefly before closing the door behind her.

A million thoughts raced through her mind, trying to break free on the surface. How the hell did he get into her room? Did he find the money? The drugs? Her eyes darted around the room, searching her secret hiding places, before her gaze dropped to the floor, avoiding eye contact. She started humming numbers backward from one hundred.

"What's the matter, cat got your tongue?" He grinned and flashed her a mouth full of gold-plated teeth.

"What do you want?"

"You been running around here for days disrespecting the order of things, so I felt it was time for us to have a little conversation."

"How did you get in my room?" The humming grew louder. The crazy sneaking up on her. Both his crisp white tennis shoes were planted firmly on the floor, but he leaned back on her bed, then propped himself up on his elbows. He eyed her suspiciously. "I guess you haven't figured out that every room here is Ray's room," he said, eyeing her suspiciously. "Yo, why the fuck you humming like that?"

"I need you to get the fuck out of my room," she barked.

The sleazy motel pimp grabbed her wrist and slammed her on the bed. Her familiar script came quick and choppy.

"Please don't hurt me. I'll do anything you want, I-I just need to go freshen up—"

"How long did you think I was going to let your ass prance around here without giving me a taste? You don't need to freshen up nothing. I like my meat with a little salt on it," he said. "I'm about to put that humming you doing to good use!" he said, licking her neck.

Austyn tried harder to get away, but his body weight held her motionless beneath him. A car door slammed, followed by loud, angry voices, which could be heard in the parking lot.

"What the hell?"

He got up off her, held the waist of his sagging pants, and walked the short distance to the window. He peeked outside, then quickly began fastening his belt buckle.

"I need you to bring your ass down to my room in fifteen minutes. Not a moment sooner or later. And don't make me have to come back and get you either."

As soon as the door closed, she placed the safety chain on the door and stood there a moment with her back pressed against it. She had to get out of there. Without a trace of emotion, she scrambled to the closet, removed the floorboard, and exhaled a sigh of relief when she saw the black duffel bag. She picked it up and tossed it on the bed, then with lightning speed, she scrambled to collect the rest of her belongings.

Once the car was packed, Austyn spent a few minutes pacing the floor, figuring out what she was going to do and how she was going to do it. Her hands shook a little as she knelt down in front of the air-conditioning unit and located the familiar bump she was looking for.

She opened her kit, took out a syringe, and filled it with the clear liquid from two of the tiny bottles. Normally, it only took five cc's to do the trick, but ten cc's seemed appropriate. Out of habit, she flicked the round cylinder to remove the air bubbles, but she caught herself and laughed. For this patient, it didn't matter if air was in the syringe or not, because complications with his heart and circulatory system would be the least of his worries.

After taking one last look around, she rezipped the small bag, then carefully tucked the syringe up the sleeve of her sweatshirt. It was time to put her full plan into motion. But first, she had to go pay Ray a visit.

With the courtyard empty, Austyn made her way to the room at the far end of the building. The door was slightly ajar, and she found Ray perched on the bed with nothing on but boxer briefs and a thick gold chain.

"Close the door and lock it behind you." He called to someone in the bathroom, "Baby girl, c'mere."

Austyn was startled when a young girl who looked to be around sixteen years old eased out of the bathroom. She was wearing denim shorts, blinged-out sneakers, and a safety-orange T-shirt. Austyn felt like she was staring at an image of her fourteen-year-old self. The young girl looked terrified, her eyes swollen and red like she'd been crying. Austyn understood exactly what she was going through. Her mind transported back to strangers using her body for their pleasure, and then disregarding her like she was trash. Men like Ray.

"I was beginning to think you stood me and Cherry—"

"My name is Najee!" the young girl yelled and began to cry uncontrollably. "I've been kidnapped, and I want to go home," she managed between sobs.

"Shut the fuck up. I told you your name is Cherry and this is your home now—until Daddy pops that cherry, then I'm sending you to Vegas."

"I don't do children," Austyn said, allowing the hidden syringe to slide into the palm of her hand.

"I need Cherry to understand how to give and receive pleasure from both a man and a woman. And once she learns the ropes, she's gonna make me a lot of money. Ain't that right, Cherry?"

Austyn began to unravel from the inside out. A heavy feeling rested in her chest. The young girl's sad eyes caught Austyn's and pleaded for help.

"Lose the girl or I'm outta—"

Within seconds, Ray was out of the bed, his hand wrapped around her throat. This felt like a repeat of the scene from her room, but this time she wanted it, needed him close in order for her plan to work. His eyes hardened.

"Bitch, you ain't controlling nothing in here," he said, looking over his shoulder at Najee, then back at her. "Now both you bitches, get fucking undressed."

The girl bolted back into the bathroom, slammed the door, and locked it behind her.

Do it now, the voice in Austyn's brain echoed. She eased the cap off the syringe and waited for the opportunity.

"Cherry! Cherry! Goddammit, get yo ass back out here now!" He waited a few beats, but the door never opened. "After I teach this bitch a lesson about Ray's world, you're next!"

Using the distraction, Austyn raised her free arm in the air and jabbed him in his neck, injecting the clear liquid in one fluid motion, then dropped the syringe on the floor. Ray's eyes bulged in surprise. He released her, his hand now searching for the pinch that he'd just felt on his neck.

"Bitch! What did you give me?"

Ray pushed her back so hard her body slammed, then bounced on the bed. Austyn scrambled toward the wooden headboard to give space as she removed the scalpel from the front pocket of the hoodie. Ray lunged and she attacked, the first slice cutting Ray across the cheek.

He reached for the sting on his face, and bright red blood seeped through his fingers.

"Fuck! You cut my face," Ray cried out in disbelief. "You crazy bitch, I'ma kill you." His movements were quick at first, but quickly slowed, unable to control the drug-induced sluggishness that was spreading through his body. He fell back on the bed, searching her face for answers.

"What the fuck did you give me?" he slurred.

"Something to rid the world of your misery."

With the medication in full control, Austyn cut him again

and again—payback for every sick bastard who had ever done her wrong. Then, instead of her usual modus operandi, she slit his throat in one quick swipe, and watched closely as the life seeped out of him.

"Who's the bitch now, you fucking predator!"

Najee sat crouched on the bathroom floor, terrified by the sounds seeping under the locked door. She had to get out of there before they came back for her. Sobbing quietly and hoping not to attract attention, she chastised herself as the meeting with the man on Bay Street flashed through her mind. How could she be so stupid to believe his story about some modeling job? She knew better than that. She needed Tony to know she was smarter than that. Still sluggish from whatever drug they gave to her, her eyes bounced around the confined space, spotting the small rectangular window up above. It was dark outside, but this was her only chance. Before she could push herself into the upright position, she heard footsteps coming toward the closed door, and she bolted upright and yanked back the shower curtain. Her heart sank and the tears flowed instantly. There was no way she could fit through the window, but maybe she could scream for help and help would come for her. There was a quick knock.

"Hey."

Najee looked back at the locked door, her breaths coming fast and quick. She was on the verge of hyperventilation.

"He can't hurt you anymore, but don't open this door for anyone until the police come."

Najee remained silent. Was this a trick? Where were the other guys who brought her here in the first place?

"Do you hear me?" the woman's voice said again.

"How long before they come?"

"I don't know, but don't forget what I said."

CHAPTER 33

The twenty-room motel was situated on the main street that ran through Pittsburg. Reporters had the property under siege as police officers from multiple agencies fought to secure the crime scene. As he drove past, Donathan could see the yellow caution tape fluttering in the wind at the far end of the property.

He parked across the street, next to the light-blue Toyota Corolla, and stepped out of his Mercedes, tugging on the bib of the baseball cap he'd worn to help shield his identity. He knew there would be reporters present, and the last thing he needed was for the media frenzy to focus on his presence. He adjusted his sunglasses and stood next to the private investigator, a barrage of questions firing from his mouth.

"What the hell is going on? I can't believe you found Austyn and Lois Greene. Why didn't you call me last night?"

Never taking his eyes off the scene unfolding across the street, Holsey snapped. "Let's get something clear right now. I don't only work for you. You are paying me to locate Lois Greene, not Austyn Greene. Now, if I were you, I'd be quiet and grateful that you're here."

A police car drove up and blocked the lane of traffic closest to the motel entrance. The uniformed officer exited the cruiser and directed the traffic to a single lane.

"Follow me and zip it," the old man said, his voice sounding gravelly, like sandpaper.

Donathan followed behind the man, inhaling the thirdhand smoke as it drifted off the private detective's clothing. Chain-smoking inside confined cars and being exposed to carbon dioxide had visibly caught up with him. His orange leathery skin was the worst thing Donathan had ever seen. They jaywalked across the four lanes of traffic and weaved to the front of the chaos. Holsey called to one of the detectives, and he motioned for the officer standing guard to let him in.

"He's with me," he said, motioning to Donathan as they ducked under the crime scene tape and made their way over to the officer who looked like he was in charge.

"Detective McGrady," Holsey said. "What's the story?"

"The deceased is Raymond Michael Carter. He's been arrested for minor drug possessions and a few assaults, but it looks like he moved on to trafficking the young ladies," he said. "We found a young girl locked in the bathroom."

"Open and shut?"

"Not a speck of blood on her, but she's so traumatized she's not talking."

"Is that her in the back of the squad car?" Holsey asked, nodding his head in the direction of the crying young woman.

"The victim was transported by the Sexual Assault Response Team to John Muir Medical Center in Walnut Creek. According to the girl in the back seat, she'd gone to his room to give him some money, but when she got no answer, she used a key she had for emergencies. That's when she found him."

"How long has he been dead?"

"Twelve hours tops, but as you can see, we're not getting very much out of her right now."

"Can we take a peek at the crime scene?" asked Holsey.

The officer looked from Holsey to Donathan, then back to Holsey again.

"He's cool—"

"I know exactly who he is. Hell, anybody with a television does, too. What I'm trying to figure out is, why's he here?"

"He's helping me on a case."

Detective McGrady stared at the two men in silence for a moment longer, then said, "Let me see if I can arrange that. But the best I can do is allow you to take a look from the doorway."

Donathan surveyed the courtyard as they waited for the crime team to wave them down. Officers were going door to door, questioning the occupants, who were standing outside their rooms watching the drama unfold. It seemed that everybody was claiming not to have seen anything, but Donathan wasn't buying it. He observed as Detective McGrady began to question a tall, slender man through a partially open door. Donathan wasn't close enough to hear the man's responses, but as a therapist, he was trained to read body language. Keeping the door partially closed indicated he was hiding something.

Donathan had the urge to move closer, but then changed his mind. He was so close to finding Austyn Greene and didn't want to jeopardize the fact that Holsey had gotten him access to her last known whereabouts. He scanned the courtyard, again noting good visibility from almost any vantage point. These people might not be talking, but he'd bet money that somebody here saw or heard something.

CHAPTER 34

Sheldon hid behind the half-opened door, trying to make sense of what the detective was saying. Inside, his anxiety was teetering. He was mesmerized and terrified at the same time by the yellow caution tape separating the familiar room from everything else. Last night he'd held up in his room getting high, but on more than one occasion the commotion from the courtyard summoned him to peek out the front window. He'd seen them pull the young girl from the car kicking and screaming, but having seen that scenario play out many times before, he shrugged it off. But the thing that struck him most of the night was seeing Ray hurry out of the bitch's room then her march down to his. He didn't know much about her, but he knew enough to know that those two were like oil and water that didn't mix. Now she was dead.

"Mr. Jones, were you in your room last night?"

"I ain't did nothing," Sheldon blurted out, his heart racing like it was going to jump from his chest. He glanced over at the smoldering paraphernalia on the table and held on to the door a little tighter.

"Now, hold on," Detective McGrady said, motioning with the palms of his hands. "Nobody said you did anything."

Sheldon tried to keep a straight face. He could barely contain his glee that his prayers had been answered. Over the past few days, her impromptu conversations had kept his drug habit supplied, but he knew she was bad news and had racked his brain relentlessly trying to figure out how to escape her grasp. Turns out Ray of all people had done the deed for him. He didn't feel an ounce of remorse that the heifer was dead. His only regret was he'd have to find a new way to get his fix.

"Did you see or hear anything?" Detective McGrady asked.

Normally when Sheldon got high, sound was magnified, and last night was no different. His brain was a little fuzzy, but he'd seen her going to the room that was now covered in caution tape. But a snitch violated the code of the street, so he wasn't telling the cops a damn thing.

"I didn't see nothing."

"Did you hear anything?" the detective said with a Southern drawl.

"I didn't hear nothing either."

The detective stared at him suspiciously, then handed him a business card.

"Here's my contact information. Ray deserves justice, and finding his killer is the first part of that. But we're going to need some help. So, if anybody decides to talk," he said emphasizing the word *anybody*, "tell them to call me."

Sheldon snatched the card and slammed the door shut. He could feel bile rising in his throat. Ray? Oh, Lawd Jesus! The girl wasn't dead like he thought. She had killed Ray. He grabbed his pipe, cell phone, and backpack, and then stalked the parking lot from the shadows of the window curtains. As soon as McGrady disappeared into the taped-off room, Sheldon slipped out the door, eased past the crowd, and headed south on Railroad Avenue.

The ringing phone jolted Payton awake from her sex-induced slumber. Tony was gone, but she still felt the tingles and sensations he'd induced strumming through her body. On the drive to her condo, she couldn't keep her hands off him, and once they were inside her condo, he wasted no time. It was like he had a point to prove, and she loved every thrust of it. Later, they'd gone out to retrieve her car and come back for seconds. She couldn't believe she'd allowed him to sleep in her bed all night and hadn't gotten claustrophobic. Now he'd only been gone an hour, and she already craved his body heat in her bed.

She blew out a satisfied breath and picked up the receiver.

"Hello?"

"She killed him! She killed him," Sheldon screamed, his words rolling on top of each other.

"Slow down, Uncle Sheldon. Who killed whom?"

"That scheming bitch across the courtyard. She killed Ray, and she probably gon' kill me. Niecy, you gotta help me."

Payton sat up, her back resting against the headboard. Lord, why didn't she check the caller ID before picking up the receiver? She might not have been able to let the call go to voice mail, but at least she could have prepared herself mentally for what was to come.

"Slow down, Uncle Sheldon."

"Girl, listen. She killed Ray, and she's after you and Lois!"

"Who killed somebody?" she questioned, trying to connect the dots playing peek-a-boo on the fringes of her mind. Although her uncle had a serious drug problem, his bold personality and addictive charms attracted the wrong crowd. Payton warned him many times that he had to be careful on the streets. Now it sounded like he'd gotten himself mixed up in a murder. But she didn't understand why the name sounded vaguely familiar.

At first, the memory was fuzzy, then suddenly it came to her.

"The pimp at your motel?" Payton said, sitting more upright in bed.

Yesterday, Ray—well, at least that's what she thought he said his name was—had been alive and well, shaking her down for money. If his no-good ass was dead, she didn't feel the least bit sorry, but she didn't want her uncle to go to prison for something like this.

"Yes! That's what I've been trying to tell you."

"Did you hurt someone, Uncle Sheldon?" she asked, growing more concerned. His paranoid rant was over the top, and she had to convince him to get some help so she could get to the bottom of this. Payton opened her nightstand drawer and reached for a notepad with information about a drug detox center in Concord. A few days ago, she'd called to inquire about the process to get someone into rehab, and now she was glad she did. "Where are you?"

"Jack in the Box on Railroad."

"Stay there, I'm on my way."

The drive to Pittsburg went by quickly. Payton was desperate to pick up Sheldon and get him to the facility where he could get help. Only then would they be able to have a lucid conversation. But she had her work cut out for her because the first obstacle was to convince him to go. When she arrived at the fast-food chain, she had no idea what state she would find him in. She went inside, looked around, and just as she'd feared, there was no sign of Sheldon. She pushed open the restroom door and called out to him, but there was no answer.

"Fuck, fuck, fuck!" she mumbled under her breath. He could be anywhere, and she had no idea where to look first. "This is the last time I'm falling for this shit." When she reached her car door, she heard the faint sound of the nickname only he called her in the distance. "Niecy. Niecy," he hissed.

Payton spun around, searching for where the voice was coming from.

"Niecy," she heard again.

Her eyes traveled along the back fencing, and she did a double take when a crouching figure came into focus.

"Uncle Sheldon!"

"Shhhhh," he said, turning a full 360 degrees, his arms flapping wildly in the air.

She shook her head and closed the distance between them, now aggravated by his foolishness. His hands trembled profusely as he lit a cigarette, took a long drag, and blew out a constant stream of smoke, the crumbling ashes fluttering to the ground. "Since when did you start smoking?"

"Why you all up in my business?"

"Uncle Sheldon, I don't have time for your shenanigans right now. Are you high?"

He squatted down quickly. "Don't say my name," he hissed. "She could be listening."

Payton glanced over her shoulder, then focused her attention back on her uncle. His behavior at the moment warranted a mental health professional, not rehab. Maybe then she would get a glimpse of the man who had spoiled her rotten in her teen years. Right now, the roles were definitely reversed, and she was exhausted from caring for a grown-ass man with these sporadic episodes that caused him to behave like a child. The problem was that her drug-addicted uncle had been smoking crack for well over ten years, and all she could do was pray that the crack had not permanently fried his brain.

"Uncle Sheldon, settle down and tell me what this is about again," she said softly.

Avoiding eye contact, he blew out another long stream of smoke before he responded.

"Girl, if I didn't know any better, I'd swear you were as dumb as a box of rocks, but I helped pay for your education, so I know that's a lie. I already told you what this was about over the phone. Now, can we go?"

"I know you did, but I just want to make sure I fully understand all the details."

Payton reached for his arm, the distinct smell of burnt rubber jolting her back to her childhood with Lois. She snickered at the irony. Why her? Out of all the things she had to deal with, why was this man her cross to bear?

"So, you think this is a joke?" he said, crushing out his cigarette.

"Look, why don't we go back to your room? You can shower, grab a few things, and—"

"I ain't going back to that death trap. They got the room blocked off with yellow tape, and the cop said he's dead." Sheldon reached into his pocket and fumbled with the cigarette pack.

"What the fuck!" Payton muttered. "So, why is the prostitute after you, again?"

"Prostitute? She ain't no damn prostitute. That heffa is a dope-pushing killa!"

Payton took a deep breath, willed herself to stay calm. She'd been in denial for months, but that all stopped right now. This was much worse than she thought, and she had an obligation to help. Her uncle loved his freedom and would fight tooth and nail before he gave that up, but today was the day that Sheldon Jones was going to detox, and she didn't care if he wanted to go or not. Then, once he was clean and sober for a few days, they could have a discussion about some serious life changes he needed to make.

"Don't light that. C'mon."

"Where we going?" he whispered.

"Just c'mon."

CHAPTER 35

As Payton waited at the stoplight to turn onto Highway 4, she noticed a lot of chaos in front of the motel. Police cars, fire trucks, and hordes of people crowded the sidewalk. What was going on down there? She glanced over at her uncle, who seemed to be holding his breath. There were stains all over his jacket, and he looked tired and worn out, but maybe he wasn't as crazy as she believed, after all. When the light turned green, instead of merging onto the highway, Payton jerked the car into the flow of traffic.

"What the hell are you doing?"

After realizing there was no immediate escape, Sheldon quickly unbuckled his seat belt and crouched lower in the passenger seat, trying to hide himself from view.

"Get up from there," Payton said, shaking her head at her uncle. She glanced into the courtyard and spotted a man who looked familiar. He wore a black baseball cap and aviator sunglasses to hide his identity, but when she spotted his car parked across the street, her suspicions were confirmed. Why was Donathan here? She pulled into the lot and parked parallel to his vehicle, giving Sheldon a clear vantage point of the action taking place across the street. She turned off the engine and hesitated before removing the car key.

"Stay put. I'm locking you inside, and if you open the door, the alarm will sound."

Before Sheldon could respond, Payton was out of the car, the door slamming behind her. With the windows sealed tight, the beads of sweat appeared instantly.

A screaming alarm would bring unwanted attention, and he didn't want to go to jail. He waited a few minutes before he raised his head to get a better view. There were more cops now, and a white van with *Coroner* written on the side was parked in the middle of the lot. His eyes widened when he saw Payton talking to the tall black man he'd made eye contact with when he was making his getaway. The man looked in his direction, and Sheldon quickly ducked out of sight.

"Got dammit," he cursed. That heifer was colluding with the enemy.

He should have never called her in the first place. If she would just give him his share of the money, he could disappear and live his life the way he wanted to. Now she was trying to get him locked up. Frantically, Sheldon yanked at the door handle, alternating between pushing and pulling, but it didn't budge. Before he could locate the Unlock button, Payton and the man were standing outside the car. He heard a soft thud, followed by the opening of the rear passenger door as the man slid inside.

"Let me outta this car!" Sheldon yelled. "I ain't talking to no damn police." He fidgeted with door buttons, this time finding the power lock. He released the lock, but Payton locked the door again. She coughed.

"Damn, you need a bath!"

Sheldon narrowed his gaze on her as she jammed the key into the ignition, opened the sunroof, and turned the air-conditioning on full blast.

"Girl, I'm not playing with you. Let me out of this damn car!"

"Calm the hell down," she said in disbelief. "He's—"

"I don't give a damn who he is, you conniving bitch! You just want me to go to jail so you can take my money."

"'Bitch'? You think I put up with all the shit you do for some goddamn money? Have you lost your fucking mind?"

Sheldon felt the man's hand touch his shoulder, and he shrugged it away. "Get yo hands off of me! I ain't no snitch, and I ain't talking to no damn police."

"I'm not a cop, Sheldon. I'm a doctor."

Sheldon stopped moving and angled his body to face him.

"Payton, what the hell is going on?" he screamed. "How much are you paying him to say I'm crazy so you can take my money?"

"Will you stop it already about that damn money? I hate to burst your bubble, but there is not enough money in the world to pay me for your bullshit. This is fucking serious. I believe the woman who murdered the man across the street is Austyn Greene. And I believe she's my half sister."

"You ain't got no sisters! You are my brother's only child, and Lois ain't said nothing about having another daughter."

Even as he said the words, it suddenly became clear. Lois was a good-for-nothing, lying bitch who was always angling for herself, and he should have known she was up to something. But what?

Sheldon was silent a moment, digesting his realization. This explained why that crazy girl was so fixated on Payton and Lois.

"Did you ever go inside her room for anything?" Donathan asked.

"No," he said in a trancelike state. "But last night, I saw her go into Ray's room. Then this morning, I saw them bringing that young girl out."

"Look, Sheldon. You have to help us stop her. Austyn is dangerous. If we don't find her soon, I'm afraid she's going to hurt somebody else."

"I don't see what I can do," he said matter-of-factly. "I told you everything I know. I mean, the last time she came to my room, she wanted me to tell her where Lois was. Said if I did, she'd give me something, but—"

"Do you know where Lois is?" Donathan questioned.

Sheldon hesitated, reluctant to say a single word. He couldn't believe Lois had been playing him for a fool when he'd been nothing but good to her, even talked his brother into allowing her to stay in the basement of the house. He didn't know Lois's exact whereabouts, but he knew enough to help them find her. And when they did locate her, he couldn't wait to find out what her scheming ass was really up to. She probably double-crossed that other girl, which is why she was so desperate to find her.

"The girl put her number in my phone," he said, reaching into his jacket pocket to retrieve the palm-sized device. He pressed a few buttons, then scrolled through his contacts, settling on *Dr. Feel Good,* the one name that stood out from the five numbers he'd saved to the cell phone himself.

"This is her number right here."

As Payton stared at the name, her face flooded with disbelief.

"We could set up a fake meeting," Donathan said. "Use Lois as bait. The private investigator I hired said Lois was staying at a rehabilitation house not too far from here, and he took pictures of Austyn snooping around the place last night. Let me go get the address."

Payton and Sheldon watched in silence as Donathan jogged across the street and disappeared into the sea of reporters.

"Does he even need to go get the address?"

Sheldon shrugged his shoulders.

"You know exactly where she is, don't you?"

"Um . . . well, not exactly. I mean, the last time I saw Sonya, I mean Lois, was that day at the courthouse when the judge sentenced her to rehab for passing bad checks," he stuttered.

"Sonya? Checks? Wait one damn minute. Are you telling me that Sonya Mitchell and Lois Greene are one and the same?"

Silence.

"Answer me, dammit! I can't believe you've been lying to me all this time. No matter what time of day or night you call me, I come running, and this is how you repay me?"

Sheldon kept his eyes downward, too embarrassed to look her in the eye. He'd gone along with Lois's plan to use the alias Sonya Mitchell for reasons of his own. The longer she squatted in the basement, the longer it would take for Payton to sell his childhood home. All along, he'd been dropping hints that Lois was back in town, but never in his wildest dreams did he imagine that Lois's presence would put his niece in danger.

Payton handed him back his cell phone. "I think it's time we give *Dr. Feel Good* a call to arrange a little meeting."

Sheldon gave her a quizzical look. "You wasting your time, that girl ain't gonna talk to you. She too damn sneaky and way too smart for that."

"I totally agree, but that's perfectly fine, since I'm not the one who is going to make the call. You are."

"What?" Sheldon said, thinking about how manipulative and evil Austyn was. She had killed many men, including Ray, so his best bet was to keep his damn mouth shut. He had already blabbed his mouth enough. He shook his head profusely.

"I ain't calling no damn body."

"Make the call, and I'll give you your share of the money with no strings attached."

CHAPTER 36

Sitting upright in the back seat of the Nissan, Austyn shielded her eyes from the harshness of the sun. It was the weekend, and she'd parked the car in the deserted warehouse district, hoping the cops or anybody else wouldn't find her. In the few hours since she'd left the motel, she was conflicted. Half of her wanted to run back to Los Angeles and put this all behind her. The other half knew she couldn't leave without finishing what she came here to do. Kill Lois.

Fueled by pure adrenaline, she studied her fingernails, and for the first time noticed traces of blood dried around her cuticles. She grabbed the bottle of water from the passenger seat, opened the door, and doused it all over her hands. She rubbed them together vigorously, the enormity of what she'd done washing over her.

"Nobody is ever gonna hurt me again, nobody is ever gonna hurt me again, nobody is ever gonna hurt me again."

Austyn closed her eyes tightly, tried to pretend she was in a safe place back in Los Angeles, but all she could think of was Lois. Once she made her pay for what she'd done to her, then she could go home.

A high-pitched shrill coming from her pay-as-you-go cell phone startled her. She quickly picked it up, her eyes trying to focus on the screen. She stared at the blocked number as the phone rang and rang. Nobody had this number, so the call was probably for the previous owner of the recycled number. The ringing finally stopped, and just as she was about to return the phone to the cup holder, it started to ring again. This time she answered.

"Hello."

"I need a little something."

"You have the wrong number—"

"Wait, don't hang up!"

"Who is this?" she said, her pulse quickening.

"Sheldon."

"How did you get this number?"

"These fucking cops ova here beating on doors. Got my damn nerves on edge. I need a little something—"

"Who gave you my fucking number?" she questioned, trying to get her bearings. The police already found the body? She'd hoped that wouldn't happen for a few more days. Now it was only a matter of time before they were hot on her trail.

"C'mon, don't make me beg," he said, sounding desperate. "You got that good shit, and all I need is one baggie—"

"What the fuck does that have to do with me?" she snapped.

"You said if I set you up with Lois, you'd hook me up. Does that ring any damn bells?"

"Lose this number—"

"Austyn, wait!"

"What did you just call me?"

"I-I-I know where Lois is."

Austyn's breathing was slow and measured. Nobody in that shithole knew who the fuck she was, and she definitely hadn't told anyone her name, especially not his crackhead ass. He was probably over there singing like a bird.

"Who the hell told you my name?"

"I-I-I—"

"Never mind. I don't need you to tell me shit. You should have just kept your mouth wrapped around that pipe and out of my damn business," she said, her temper exploding. "Now, after I take care of Lois, I'm coming back for your big-mouth ass!"

She jumped out of the car and slammed the cheap cell phone into the pavement, breaking the device into a thousand tiny pieces.

"Fuck!" she screamed at the top of her lungs, then slid into the driver's seat, cranked the engine, and headed toward Glover House to finish what she had come here to do. She crawled along at the speed limit, keeping a sharp watch for the police or anyone who looked suspicious.

A few minutes later, Austyn parked the car next to the curb on the quiet suburban street. Just as she'd done a few nights ago. She checked her watch. It was almost noon, the time of day when most of the women were volunteering at the soup kitchen. If Lois was in the house, now was the perfect time to make her move.

She reached her sweaty palm under the front seat, wrapped her hand around the cold piece of steel, and lifted the heavy revolver she'd taken from Ray's room to her lap. She fondled the pistol, feeling powerful and in control.

"Ready or not, Lois, here I come."

CHAPTER 37

The two-story house looked ordinary in the light of day. A typical suburban home nestled in the court with others like it. Austyn rang the doorbell, then thrust both hands deep into the front pocket of her hoodie.

An older woman opened the front door.

"Good afternoon, may I help you?" she said in a slight British accent.

"I'm here to see Lois Greene."

The woman's eyes widened with concern, but she held Austyn's gaze. "I'm sorry, but we don't—"

"You don't what?" Austyn pulled the gun from her front pocket and aimed it at the woman. "Say one word, and I'll kill you dead. Do you understand me?"

Austyn stepped into the foyer and closed the door behind her. "Are you the only one here?"

The woman nodded.

"Where is she?"

The woman jutted her chin toward the stairs.

"Is she alone?"

The woman nodded.

★　★　★

After securing the woman to an office chair using packing tape, Austyn wrapped several more revolutions of the clear adhesive around the woman's mouth.

After climbing the stairs, Austyn opened the closed bedroom doors one by one. Finally, she found a woman in her late fifties sprawled facedown on the bed.

"Get up, you bitch!" Austyn spat, waving the gun at Lois. "I bet you never thought you'd see me again."

Lois Greene rolled over and gingerly pushed herself upright on the twin bed. The whites of her eyes and skin were jaundiced, and the woman's face sagged with confusion.

"Do I know you? 'Cause I ain't got no beef with you."

"So now you want to act like you have amnesia? Bitch, I wasn't born yesterday," Austyn said, brandishing the gun.

"Look, I-I think you have me confused with someone else. I haven't lived here in years."

"I know exactly who you are. Lois. Anne. Greene. Born to a two-dollar whore who fucked so many men she had no clue who yo daddy is. The bitch who no one wanted so she sold the innocence of her eight-year-old daughter to feed her crack addiction."

Lois stared at Austyn like she'd seen a ghost.

"You are the goddamn monster who watched, even cheered on, the many men who climbed on top of that helpless little girl without remorse. The heartless bitch who ruined my fucking life. Does that ring any bells?"

Fear and recognition of the woman brandishing the gun in front of her washed over Lois Greene's face. She shifted on the bed as if the mere sound of her own breathing would set off a volatile chain of events. Austyn moved in closer, placed the barrel of the gun against Lois's forehead.

"Say something, you heartless bitch! When I close my eyes, not only do I see them—I see you. How could you do that? I was a little girl. Mothers are supposed to protect their children!"

Austyn switched the gun to her left hand, then removed the surgical blade from the front pocket on her hooded sweatshirt.

"Say something! Say something, you whore!"

Lois closed her eyes, refused to utter a single word, hoping her demise would come painless and quick. But as fast as the cold steel had been placed between her eyes, it was removed. Her eyes shot wide open just in time to anticipate the first slice.

"A gunshot would be too easy for you. I want you to feel every bit of this!"

CHAPTER 38

Sydney smiled at her reflection in the rearview mirror as she parked her car in one of the spots reserved for doctors. She turned off the engine and listened to Donathan's smooth baritone voice as he recited a promotional spot for his impending return to the airwaves later in the week. His low, sexy rumble was conjuring up erotic thoughts, which was not something they'd entertained or indulged in over the past few days.

Professionally, things were looking up for the Jameses. She'd just returned from the hand surgeon and had been cleared for minor surgeries. It wasn't total operating room carte blanche yet, but she was happy to be back in the game. And as of this morning, Donathan was seeing patients again. But personally, they needed some serious work.

Neither had spoken more than two unnecessary words to one another since the incident at Pican's, and she was exhausted trying to manage his moods. If she could just get him to move past his suspicions about Miles, everything would go back to the way it used to be. Sydney thought about it a moment. That was a lie and she knew it, but at least it was a start. For obvious reasons, she rarely took marriage advice from Payton, but for once they were in agreement on how to handle the situation, which was to take this secret to the grave. Right now, her number-one priority was to get Donathan to let go of what he believed to be true once and for all. She grabbed her handbag off the passenger seat and hurried toward the hospital entrance, but before she reached the sliding glass doors, Miles exited the building toward her.

"You're late, Dr. James," he said, flashing that million-dollar smile.

"Well, this is a surprise," she said easily. "What are you still doing here?"

"We had another emergency and needed all hands on deck, but everything is under control now."

"Well, I'm almost free and clear to carry my own weight again," she said, holding up the palm of her hand, exposing the flesh-colored bandage. She couldn't help noticing how his gaze roamed up and down her body before zeroing back on her eyes with target-like precision.

Miles raised an eyebrow and half-smiled. "It's not a problem. That's what friends are for, right?"

With every fiber of her being, she wanted to consider Miles her friend, but if she couldn't control her thoughts, how could continuing their friendship be possible? But then again, maybe if she convinced Miles to help her out with her plan, then her marriage would get back on track and she could get back to not even looking at, much less thinking about, another man. If Donathan heard it—once and for all—from Miles, that nothing happened between them, maybe they could move on. "Is everything alright?" he questioned.

Sydney hesitated. "Yes, but there's something I need to talk to you about."

"I'm listening."

She glanced over his shoulder and noticed the security guard, Albert, looking their way. Gossiping tongues were in overdrive since she and Miles had both returned to work, and the last thing she wanted to do was fan the flames. She also didn't want to end up in the local internet gossip rag like Donathan. She glanced around for a sighting of anyone who looked like they didn't belong. "You two just can't seem to keep your hands off one another."

Sydney recognized the familiar voice immediately. Julia Stevens. She was sick and tired of this red-haired bitch being in her business. Once and for all, she needed to put this heffa in her place. As if reading her mind, Miles shook his head.

"Look, I need to ask you a huge favor."

"I'm listening."

"Not here. Can I stop by your loft when I get off later?"

CHAPTER 39

Perched next to a window overlooking Broadway, Miles surveyed the people walking by. He was tired, but too wound up to sleep. He'd run almost ten miles on the treadmill and took a long, hot shower, but his mind wouldn't shut off. Instead it toyed with different scenarios. What type of favor did Sydney want from him? He was just about to dig into his combo plate when he received the call.

"Are you home?" Sydney asked, her voice a lot less sure than it was when she'd proposed this meeting a few hours ago.

"I can be by the time you get here."

"Look, I didn't think about this earlier, but you've worked a long shift and you're probably exhausted. Maybe, we can just do this another—"

"I'll let the doorman know you're coming," he said and ended the call before she could change her mind. He motioned for his server to come back to the table.

"Is everything alright, Dr. Day?"

"Gotta take it to go."

"No problem. Let me wrap this up for you," the young black man said, removing the plate of barbecue chicken and link sausages from in front of him.

Within minutes, the young man returned with a to-go container packed in a plastic bag and handed it to Miles, who took the food in exchange for two crisp folded bills, which was more than enough to pay for his food and leave a sizable tip. He slipped on his jacket and hurried toward the side door.

"Thanks for always taking care of me, Rich," he called over his shoulder.

During his short walk across the street, Miles's thoughts repeatedly turned to Sydney, to the question of what she needed to talk to him about.

By the time he reached the concierge desk in his condominium, his curiosity was in overdrive. He left Sydney's name with the doorman and continued his long strides toward the elevator, wondering what had happened to change her mind. When he asked her before to meet him here to talk, she had declined. So why now?

Sydney stepped off the elevator and saw Miles leaning against his doorway talking on his cell phone. Miles smiled, and her pulse quickened as he held her gaze. Her eyes studied him, and for the first time in weeks, she looked as long as she wanted without fear of being caught by some onlooker who would try to interpret what she was thinking.

His dreadlocks framed his face, and his black jeans and T-shirt made him look sexy and dangerous.

Once she reached him, he stepped into the hallway, allowing her to enter first, then closed the door behind them. He motioned for her to have a seat. Sydney made her way to the floor-to-ceiling window and looked out across a serrated skyline of buildings and water. Sydney stood there for a while, her eyes tracking left then right, eventually resting on the alabaster-blue rooftop of the Waterfront Hotel in the distance. She closed her eyes and fought to subdue the memory, but it teased her senses—the recollection of the cool glass pressed against her back, her hands tangled in his mass of dreads with him kneeling before her pacifying her pain. This scene replayed in her head like the loop of a pornographic movie.

The hairs quivered on the back of her neck, and a chill traced the contours of her spinal column as Miles came up behind her.

"Wine?"

Sydney turned her head to the side to face Miles, hesitating before wrapping her well-manicured fingers around the offered glass. There was an awkward silence between them, but that didn't suppress her unfocused anxiety. She resisted the irrational urge to kiss him. Maybe coming here was not a good idea after all.

"C'mon, let's have a seat."

Once she was settled on the sofa, Miles took the seat opposite her. Trying to get ahold of herself, Sydney took a huge gulp of wine. This had to be the dumbest shit she had ever done in her life. What made her think she could waltz in here and walk out unscathed? Miles leaned forward, his forearms resting on his thighs, and Sydney unconsciously leaned back. Sydney exhaled audibly and placed the glass on the table in front of them. It was now or never.

"Okay. I need to ask you a favor," she blurted, the words quickly tumbling from her mouth.

"I think we've already established that." He chuckled.

She could feel the heat as he stared at her, waiting for her to tell him what she needed.

"I need you to tell Donathan that nothing inappropriate happened between us." She looked down, unable to make eye contact, leaving her request hanging in the air.

Miles walked into his kitchen, grabbed the opened bottle of wine, and took a long swig. "Let me get this straight. You want me to go talk to your husband?" He set the bottle down.

Sydney was on her feet quick and stood facing him in the small kitchen. "No. I don't want you to go to him. I just want you to give him our agreed-upon answer if he comes to you and asks."

"What makes you think he's going to come to me and ask?"

"He's obsessed with what he thinks happened between us, and since he's not satisfied with my responses, he's threatened to come to you. And nothing good would come from that."

"Sydney, I have never been involved with another man's wife

in my life, and I never intended to be, but somehow I find myself here. Donathan is your spouse," he continued. "You love and may even like him, but I'ma keep it real. I don't. He's selfish, he's arrogant, and he believes the world revolves around him, which is a destructive combination."

He stepped away from the island and pinned her against it.

"Besides, I never kiss and tell." He waited a beat, and then moved closer, kissing her lips gently. She'd wanted to be kissed by Miles Day, and she moaned greedily as he devoured her mouth, tracing the outline of her lips with his tongue. His hands were all over her body, and she welcomed the sensations.

"If you want me to, I will stop, but you have to ask," he said, continuing his assault.

He lifted her up onto the granite countertop. Sydney scooted into him, wrapping her legs around his waist. She knew she should tell him to stop, but the rush coursing through her veins wouldn't let her. She closed her eyes and lost herself in the moment.

"Look at me."

She squeezed her eyes tighter, afraid of what would happen if she opened them.

"Look at me," he repeated.

Miles teased her lower lip, and continued down her neck.

As he peeled off her jeans and panties, Sydney caught a glimpse of her reflection in the door of the microwave oven, and she had no idea who was staring back at her. Sydney was mesmerized as he removed the condom from his back pocket and expertly rolled it on. He looked up at her.

"Is this what you want?" he asked.

She nodded slowly and prayed for her resolve to come, but as Miles palmed the cheeks of her ass and slowly inched his way inside her, it never did.

A few hours later, both Miles and Sydney were panting heavily, drenched in sweat and sprawled haphazardly across his king-sized bed. Sydney's stomach rumbled, and Miles reached lazily for her and brushed his hand across it. He rolled over and kissed her stomach, then scooted out of the bed.

"I'm being a horrible host. Let me get you something to eat."

Sydney lay quietly, watching the rotation of the ceiling fan. She tried to bask in the multiple sensations strumming through her body, but her mind wouldn't be still. She couldn't believe she had done it. Now that the deed was done, the guilt killed her mood like a wet blanket. Here she was, a married woman, and she was lying naked in another man's bed.

CHAPTER 40

Donathan followed behind the Toyota Corolla, turn for turn, with Payton and her uncle close on his tail. Once they reached a suburban street lined with rows of single-story housing, the three-car caravan came to a stop behind a late-model Ford Escort.

Donathan was on edge, his insides knotted from the realization that after weeks of searching, he was about to put an end to his sleepless nights. By helping the authorities capture Austyn Greene, he would finally be able to put an end to his nightmare. Austyn Greene had been on the loose for weeks. The threat of her showing up at any moment to harm him or Sydney had constantly gnawed at him. He removed his suit jacket and rolled the sleeves on his white dress shirt until the cuffs rested on his forearm. Glancing in his rearview mirror, he saw Payton on her cell phone.

"Holsey," he called out as he opened the car door and joined the private detective who was moving in slow motion around the empty vehicle. He leaned forward and peered through the back window.

"Is this the car she's driving?" Donathan asked, glancing at his surroundings. He squinted up at the sun beating down on his back and could feel his undershirt sticking to him. The street was lined with flat-level housing on both sides, but the circular cul-de-sac directly in front of them stood out. The stucco homes were newer and consisted of two-story and single-family dwellings.

"Which house is it?"

"The sand-colored one right there." Holsey pointed a crooked finger toward the grouping of newer two-story homes.

"Are you sure Lois is in there?"

"Yeah, I'm sure," Holsey answered.

"Well, call the police," Donathan said, taking off toward the house. "I need to stop her before she kills someone else."

"Donathan, wait a minute!" Payton yelled, finally stepping out of her vehicle.

"Stay there, and call the police," he yelled back at her.

Once Donathan entered the cul-de-sac, there wasn't a single car parked on either side of the circular street to hide his presence. He hoped Austyn was too occupied with her plan of revenge to be on the lookout for anyone. What if she hadn't made it inside the house yet? He slowed his pace to be on the safe side, becoming hyperaware of his surroundings. A few of the homes had cars in the driveway, but for the most part, it looked like people were at work.

He moved closer to the neighboring homes and used the lawns as a pathway to get closer to the residence. When he made it to the house, he looked back at Holsey and Payton, who were watching his every move. Donathan eased onto the concrete porch and crouched down below the front window, all the while listening for any sounds of movement coming from inside. Through a crack in the blinds, he could see a female taped to an office chair. He carefully pressed his face to the glass to get a better look, and when their eyes connected, he saw fear.

She squirmed frantically, tilting her head to the left, and pointed her chin upward as if she was trying to tell him something. He stared at her, but he couldn't decipher what she was trying to tell him, until he pointed a hand toward the front door. When the woman on the chair shook her head, he pointed toward the back of the house and she nodded.

Staying low, Donathan moved around the garage, carefully opening the side gate. When he came to the door leading into the garage, he twisted the knob and the door creaked open.

Donathan quickly disappeared inside the darkened garage. Using the tiny bit of daylight peeking underneath the door, he silently weighed what to do next. His goal was to get in and keep Austyn talking until the police got there.

He found the light switch and searched the garage for anything he might be able to use to protect himself, but aside from the upright freezer and two side-by-side refrigerators, the space was clean and empty.

The last time he'd tangled with Austyn Greene, he'd let his guard down and had ended up drugged and lying helpless on the floor, within inches of being castrated. But this time he was ready.

The one advantage he had right now was the element of surprise. Since Austyn's weapon of choice was to drug her victims helpless, then use a scalpel to castrate them, as long as he didn't get too close to her, he'd be fine.

Adrenaline flowing through his bloodstream, he pried the small, white rectangle sensor from the doorjamb, then pushed the door inward, praying he'd disarmed the contact and the alarm wouldn't chime.

Making his way to the room where he'd seen the woman tied up, he used a pair of desk scissors to remove the tape and released her. Once the woman confirmed that Austyn and Lois were in the house, Donathan instructed her to leave the same way he'd just come in.

Donathan took his time climbing the stairs. At the top, he followed the sound of voices.

When he reached the door in question, he heard a woman moaning in pain on the other side and burst in.

Austyn turned with a gun now pointed at him. Her hands shook violently.

Donathan lunged for the gun, yanking and twisting it, then fell on top of her. Three bullets were discharged before he wrestled the weapon free and tossed it across the room. She continued to squirm underneath him as he felt the warmth seep into the fabric of his crisp white shirt.

Before the reality of his being shot set in, the Pittsburg SWAT team swarmed the house, then disarmed and took Austyn down.

"Oh God!" Payton yelled when she heard distant gunshots. She locked eyes with Sheldon, who looked as if he'd seen a ghost. The area was now swarming with cops, and they'd blocked off the entrance into the court.

"Stay right here, Sheldon," she demanded before jumping out of the car and starting toward the cul-de-sac.

By the time she made it to the police barricade, she was panting heavily. It dawned on her that not only was Donathan in that house, but so were Austyn and Lois Greene. She shared the same blood that was running through her veins with both of them, and she could give a damn if either one of them were dead. She pushed her way through the small crowd, trying to position herself to see around the officers and trucks blocking her view. Then she was met by a familiar face.

"Detective McGrady, I have to get in there," Payton said, her voice trailing off.

"Hold on, Ms. Jones, I can't let you down there."

In the distance, Payton saw several men in black escorting a handcuffed woman down the driveway to the back of a waiting police vehicle.

"Oh God, did she shoot him?" she asked, trying to push past the detective.

"Ms. Jones, you have to stay back."

A female voice squawking through the walkie-talkie stilled her.

"African American male, early forties, multiple gunshot wounds to the abdomen. Life Flight is en route."

Payton's shoulders instantly deflated, and everything seemed to be spinning out of control around her. She could feel Detective McGrady's hands resting on her biceps, and it took her a moment before she was able to string together her next words.

"Can I go in the ambulance with him?"

"He's being airlifted to John Muir Medical Center in Walnut Creek. The best thing you can do is meet him at the hospital. Are you okay to drive?"

Two ambulances arrived at once, and several police officers moved the blockade to let them through. The whooshing of blades grew louder. Payton looked up to see a black and white helicopter coming closer. She also noticed that the paparazzi had arrived and the street was swarming with cameras.

Payton glanced toward the house again and held her breath when she saw a gurney being wheeled out the door. In the distance, the figure being wheeled out looked to be another female. She was too far away to make out her features, but one paramedic was working on her while the other was holding what looked to be an IV bag above her head.

"Ms. Jones, does your brother have a wife?" Detective McGrady asked, bringing her thoughts back to the present.

"Yes."

"I think you should call her."

CHAPTER 41

Tony checked his cell phone again, hoping to see a text message miraculously appear. How could he be so careless? He hadn't heard from Najee in over twenty-four hours and she wasn't answering her phone or responding to his text messages. Something was wrong—he could feel it in his core.

He didn't know Najee's friends, he'd never met any of their parents, and he had no clue where anybody lived. Epic fail when it came to parenting a teenager. He went into her room again, hoping to find anything that would give him a clue to her where-abouts. Not sure what he was looking for this time, he lifted the mattress, hoping to find a diary, when he noticed a business card tossed in the wastebasket. He retrieved the plain black and white rectangle and read the name embossed in script.

Dante Wilson. Photographer.

Tony's stomach tightened. What the hell did she need with a photographer?

He removed his cell phone from his jacket pocket and punched in the 925 area code, but an incoming call on the house phone stalled his attempt. He quickly grabbed the handset.

"Hello?"

"Tony?"

"Najee? Where are you? I've been calling and texting you for hours. Girl, you scared the hell out of me. Where are you?" Tony asked, relieved to finally hear her voice. "Najee? Are you there?"

There was a brief silence.

"Yes," she finally replied, her voice small, almost a whisper coming through the phone.

"Whose phone is this?"

"I don't know," she said, her words clipped and quick. "I met this guy on Bay Street. He told me he could get me some modeling jobs. I was in the Rideshare car, and then they covered my face and I couldn't breathe." She started to sob, making her words incoherent.

"Baby, don't cry. Just tell me where you are so I can come and get you."

"I'm at a hospital."

"What hospital? Is there someone there with you?"

"Yes."

"Give them the phone, please."

Tony tried to remain calm for his sister's sake, but his insides were unraveling. He waited for what seemed like an eternity before a woman's voice came on the line.

"Sir, my name is Justine Brooks and I'm with the Sexual Assault Response Task Force at John Muir Medical Center."

"Sexual assault?"

"Yes, sir. I have Najee here with me. She's safe. I need you to come to John Muir Medical Center. We're located in Walnut Creek—"

Tony ended the call and threw the cordless phone against the wall. It splintered in multiple pieces. His mother was probably turning over in her grave. She had given him one simple task, to take care of his sister, and he fucking blew it. He leaned his over-six-foot frame against the wall and outwardly wept. When he found Dante Wilson, he was going to kill him with his bare hands.

CHAPTER 42

"Tell me why you were at Glover House again?" Detective McGrady asked Payton.

They were standing in the hallway outside the trauma unit, where a team of doctors was working on Donathan. Detective McGrady was a tall man, his features well-proportioned for his medium-brown face. He was ruggedly handsome, someone Payton would have gone out with under different circumstances. But tonight he looked like she felt—tired.

"I don't mean to be rude, but I can't do this right now." Payton kept glancing at her cell phone, frustrated by the weak reception. It had been over an hour since she had phoned both Sydney and Tony, but neither had arrived yet or called.

"Ma'am, I understand that you're stressed, but we have one victim fighting for his life right now, and Ms. Mitchell, Ms. Greene, or whatever she's calling herself today, is a very sick woman who required some extensive stitching. We need answers to help us get to the bottom of this."

"Sonya Mitchell? That woman is knee-deep in criminal activity—"

"Does this have anything to do with her squatting on your property?"

Payton stared at the detective, a little suspicious by the nature of his questioning. Why would he ask her that? Did they think she was somehow involved? Once they found out that Lois and Austyn Greene were both related to her, she would become a prime suspect, too. She hesitated. "No. This has nothing to do with my property."

"Did you know that Sonya Mitchell and Lois Greene are the same person?"

"Is that her only alias?" Payton questioned without answering his.

"Probably not. People like her have multiple aliases that we don't have a clue about. Identity theft is out of control these days," the detective said, jotting something on his notepad. "I hope you didn't have anything in the house she could use to steal your identity. Her rap sheet is pretty extensive, and I'm sure she and her low-life friends are ready to prey on anyone they can. Do you know a Najee Simone Barnes?"

"She's my, umm, boyfriend's younger sister. Why are you asking?"

"It seems she got caught up in the sex trafficking ring. We found her at the motel in Pittsburg this morning locked in the bathroom of the deceased. She's not saying much, but I need to locate her family."

A wave of nausea washed over her as random thoughts flooded Payton's brain. She'd been calling Tony for the last hour and hadn't heard back from him.

"Where is she?"

"I'm not at liberty to say, but we want to reunite her with her family as soon as possible."

The word "family" hung in the air for Payton. Her grandparents taught her what the word meant. If they hadn't, she probably would have ended up just like Lois. On drugs or in jail.

"Is Najee okay?" Payton asked. She'd met Najee briefly at her mother's funeral, but she felt a certain kinship.

"Who did you say her brother was, again?"

"Anthony. Anthony Barnes. Look, Detective McGrady, I'm sorry, but I can't do this right now—"

"Criminal or not, she didn't deserve to be sliced up like that,"

Detective McGrady said, interrupting her thoughts. "I'll give you time for things to calm down, but I need you to call me as soon as your brother is out of the woods." He stood and moved to the door.

"We'll talk more later," he called after her.

Payton walked away with so many unanswered questions. She wondered exactly what her uncle Sheldon knew about all this. For months, he'd been dropping hints about Lois Greene, and whenever he talked about his friend who had been court-ordered to rehab, he never once said a name. It all made perfect sense now. Sheldon had known all along that Sonya Mitchell and Lois Greene were one and the same. Maybe that's why he'd been so nervous and disappeared during the chaos of the shooting. And exactly what did he know about the sex trafficking ring?

A few hours ago, she was practically salivating to find Lois Greene. She wanted to confront that bitch and get her out of her life once and for all. But unfortunately for Lois, her other daughter had found her first. Payton wondered if she had any other half siblings out there, and if Lois even knew that the woman who'd cut her was her daughter...

Her thoughts quickly drifted back to Donathan. He had to be okay. She wouldn't be able to live with herself knowing that her family had harmed the husband of her closest friend.

And then she thought about everybody else. Donathan and Sydney both knew that she and Austyn Greene were related. He had figured the relationship out before she had. But what would everyone else think when they found out that her half sister was the reason Donathan was fighting for his life?

She needed answers and a stiff drink to calm her nerves. But the one man who could give her those answers was probably hiding out in one of those crack dens with a glass pipe perched between his lips and wouldn't surface for a few days. But when he did, Payton would be right there to strangle his ass.

Pulling out her phone again, she headed for the bank of elevators, hoping she'd have better reception once she got out of the basement. When the doors slid open, Payton scrolled through her text messages as she made her way over to the information desk. Still nothing from Sydney or Tony.

"Is there a phone I can use?" she asked the woman seated comfortably behind the desk. The woman, wearing a pink smock with the word *Volunteer* embroidered on the left pocket, was in her late sixties, not a single strand of her classically coiffed curls out of place.

"I'm sorry, dear, but the hospital doesn't allow visitors to use the phone lines for personal use," she replied with a polite smile.

Payton started to explain, but instead turned away and headed down the long corridor toward an exit.

When she reached the parking lot, Tyrese and the Jameses were making their way toward the hospital entrance. For a brief moment she was surprised to see Tyrese, who looked forlorn and disheveled. He'd let his beard grow in, and the sweat suit he wore looked like he'd had it on for a few days. All remnants of being enmeshed in a nasty divorce. But him being there made sense; he, Tony, and Donathan were good friends. But still no sign of Tony.

Sylver James was a stark contrast to the men in her perfectly tailored red St. John suit, with a stunning multicolored scarf tossed across her shoulders.

"How is he?" Sylver asked, out of breath.

"They haven't given me any information about his condition since I arrived."

"Is Sydney with him?"

"She's on her way."

CHAPTER 43

The black Dodge Viper hummed into the parking lot. When it stopped along the curb, a frazzled Sydney jumped out. She was without makeup, dressed in jeans, and a fitted T-shirt, and her hair was pulled back into a wet ponytail. As Sydney came closer, Payton could see that her eyes were red, as if she'd been crying, and the fear on Sydney's face was palpable.

"Please tell me that he's okay," Sydney said.

"I don't know," Payton said.

"This is absurd! Malcolm, go find out what's happening to my child."

The elder Dr. James was all business as he passed a cluster of ladies smoking cigarettes and wearing T-shirts with the words *Glover House* imprinted on them. Everyone followed, including Miles, who had exited his car and appeared holding a woman's handbag. Before they reached the automatic doors, Payton turned abruptly and reached for Sydney's purse.

"I got it from here," she said, her eyes boring into his. It took Miles a minute before he reluctantly passed Payton the purse.

"I just want to make sure she's okay—"

"She's fine," Payton said, her eyes steady on Miles and clutching the black leather handbag close to her chest. This man had it bad, and if Sydney knew what was good for her, she'd stay as far away from Miles Day as possible.

"Tell her I'll call her later."

"Look, Miles. It's in everybody's best interest if you would just leave her alone."

"I don't mean any disrespect, but I'll leave her alone when she tells me to leave her alone."

Inside the emergency room waiting area, the elder Dr. James turned to his wife and said, "Wait right here." He grabbed Sydney by the hand and made his way to the front desk, where he and Sydney exchanged a few words with the nurse, then disappeared behind a set of closed double doors.

"What happened?" Tyrese asked.

"Who shot him and why were you with him?" Sylver asked.

Payton looked from one to the other as they fired a barrage of questions. She had her suspicions about what happened to Donathan in that house, but she refused to voice them out loud until she knew more. "Look," she snapped. "I know you both want answers, but I've told you everything I know."

Payton walked away, massaging her temples, trying to release the building pressure that was threatening a migraine. The antiseptic smell was making her sick, and she needed all of them to shut the hell up and quit asking her questions. Even if she wanted to say something, how the hell was she going to tell them that her half sister was the reason Donathan was on the other side of those doors fighting for his life?

Payton wanted no connection to a longtime past that she had fought so hard to escape. She just wanted to be Payton Marie Jones, not anybody's half sister or daughter, just like she had been before Lois popped back on the radar.

A few minutes later, the doors behind the intake nurse opened, and Payton noticed Detective McGrady standing next to a woman lying on a gurney parked in the hallway. The woman wore blood-stained bandages on half of her face and on both arms. That had to be Lois. Payton stared a moment, trying to remember the earliest memory of the woman who had given birth to her, but nothing registered. This woman seemed older than Payton remembered, but it was more than that. Lois used to be pretty, but this woman hadn't been pretty in a very long time. She had to be at least sixty, and from what Payton could see, the toxins of twenty-five-plus years of drug abuse had taken a toll. The whites of her eyes were a deep yellow, and from a distance her once-caramel-colored skin looked worn and leathery.

She could have walked past this woman on the street and would have had no idea that it was she who had given birth to her.

The doors closed, obstructing her view, but Payton's thoughts continued to whirl, and at that moment it occurred to her that leaving was the best gift Lois Greene could have ever given her.

The double doors through which Sydney and the elder Dr. James had gone earlier swooshed open, and Payton jerked her head in that direction, hoping it was somebody with news, but her hope quickly vanished, replaced by what felt like a lead weight settling into the pit of her stomach. Detective McGrady took deliberate strides toward her with a confused look on his face.

The closer he got, the more Payton felt like a caged animal.

"Miss Jones, Miss Jones. I need you to clarify something for me. Is it true that Lois Greene is your mother?"

Suddenly, Payton's skin felt hot and sticky all over. She couldn't believe that bitch had the audacity to refer to herself as her mother, or anybody's mother for that matter. Avoiding this very truth had been Payton's shield of protection, but there was also the hate that smoldered just beneath the surface.

Over the years, she'd imagined what she would say if the opportunity came for her to confront the woman who'd left her behind like she was a piece of trash, but Payton's practiced, rated-R words stayed trapped in her throat.

Everyone in the room, including Sylver and Tyrese, seemed to be holding their breath waiting for her to acknowledge the unthinkable.

The door behind the intake nurse opened again. This time, Payton made eye contact with the woman lying on the gurney with missing teeth and skin the color of worn Nubuck. The time had arrived to face her truth, whether she wanted to or not. She held the woman's gaze.

"Mother?" Payton replied, loud enough for everyone to hear. "That woman did give birth to me, but my mother died a very long time ago."

CHAPTER 44

Tony walked into the main lobby of John Muir Medical Center sheathed in a strong feeling of déjà vu. Over the past few weeks, he'd spent so much time in hospitals. First his mother, then Donathan after the first attack, and now both Donathan and his sister were here in this hospital. For the umpteenth time, he wanted to hit something.

He'd finally listened to his multiple voice mails from Payton telling him to get here as soon as possible because Donathan had been shot. From the way her voice sounded, things were pretty bleak and all he could do was hope for the best, but being summoned to the hospital didn't sound like good news to him. Was his best friend dead? Was that why she was so vague?

Suddenly the enormity of the situation washed over him. His best friend was somewhere in this building fighting for his life and there was a strong possibility he could be dead. Donathan and Najee both had to be okay.

He parked the car haphazardly, adrenaline propelling him through the double doors that read *Emergency Entrance*. Immediately, the subtle smells of sickness and anxiety mingled with hospital antiseptics made him nauseated. He hated being here.

In a waiting room off the main corridor, Tony noticed Tyrese, Sylver James—or Mrs. Jay, as he referred to the woman who was like a second mother to him—and Payton, who was face-to-face with a man he'd seen before, but couldn't place at the moment. He stepped inside, and Payton hurried to him, the fear in her eyes evident.

"How is he?"

"He's still in surgery."

"Sorry I couldn't get here sooner. I've been trying to find my sister—"

"Najee is here. I don't have a lot of information, but the police officer mentioned they found her at the motel in Pittsburg and she was a part of some sex trafficking ring." Before Payton could explain further, she was interrupted by the detective.

"Excuse me. Tony Barnes?"

Tony nodded.

"I'm Detective McGrady. You were contacted by the SART team—"

"Take me to my sister."

Payton grabbed Tony's hand to follow, but the detective stepped in front of her.

"I'm sorry, Ms. Jones, but only immediate family allowed."

On the elevator ride up, Tony used the confined space to get answers.

"Detective, can you please tell me what is going on, and exactly where did you find my sister?"

"She was held up in the motel room of a deceased Raymond Carter, at the Mar Ray Motel in Pittsburg," he said, referring to the name scribbled on his spiral notebook. "By chance, do you know the deceased?"

The thought of somebody violating his sister's innocence made his skin crawl. She was a goddamn baby.

"Deceased? Fuck the deceased! Look, did Najee kill this dirtbag?" he questioned, his entire body riddled with guilt. He would never be able to forgive himself for this.

"How did my sister end up at this motel? And are you saying she killed this Ray?"

"The evidence does not support that. Miss Barnes was locked in the restroom when police arrived on the scene. And good thing she was. The victim was sliced up in a way that made him unrecognizable. I've never seen anything like that before in my life," he rambled on.

"Did he hurt her?"

"From what I have gathered thus far, they drugged her to get her to the motel, but ironically, the person whom we believe did the handiwork with the scalpel actually saved your sister from a lifetime of trauma."

"Who are the 'they' who drugged her?"

"I'm working on that."

The two men exited the elevator, and Tony followed the detective to a set of secured double doors. He picked up a handset, identified himself, and they were buzzed in.

Najee ran into her brother's arms and began to sob uncontrollably. "I'm sorry! I'm sorry I didn't listen to you."

Tony hugged his sister, able to breathe a little easier. He stroked her hair and wiped away her tears, which were laced with regret that she thought she knew better. He was grateful she wasn't hurt physically, but mental trauma could sometimes be far worse. Tony sighed heavily and squeezed Najee a little tighter.

"Shhhhhh, baby girl. You're safe. I got you."

CHAPTER 45

After talking briefly with another detective, Payton located Sydney, Tyrese, and Donathan's parents in the ICU.

Tyrese and the elder James were huddled around a woman in a white lab coat.

"Mr. James came through the surgery fine, and we're expecting a full recovery. We were able to remove the bullet, but it did cause some minor damage to one of his lungs—"

"When are you going to take that tube out of his mouth?" Sylver questioned.

"Ma'am, he's only working with the capacity of one healthy lung right now, so we're keeping him on the ventilator to help him breathe a little easier. Once he wakes up, we will assess him further."

Sydney was standing next to the bed holding Donathan's hand. Payton reached out to touch Sydney's arm and noticed her lips were trembling.

"Hey, you okay?" she asked, scrutinizing her friend for a long time before wrapping her arms around her in an emotional embrace.

"I'm good," Sydney said, her voice quavering.

"Sounds like he's going to be okay."

"His vitals look good. I just want him to open his eyes," she

said, this time running a hand over his closely cropped hair. She
stilled for a moment, then asked, "Payton, what happened to my
husband?"

"C'mon, let's take a walk."

The two women left the secured wing and stepped into an
empty waiting room just off the hospital corridor. Sydney took a
seat, but Payton continued to stand, trying to process what was
going on. For a moment, half of her felt like dropping to the floor
and curling into the fetal position to quiet the noise going on inside her head. The other half wanted to tell everyone to "kiss her
black ass," as Payton was prone to say.

The detectives were relentless. Both McGrady and the other
officer seemed to be asking her the same questions over and over
again. Her pulse quickened at the possibility the detectives were
also questioning Lois, but Payton quickly reminded herself that
she had done nothing wrong. Her first instincts had been to get in
her car and drive as far away from this hospital as she possibly
could, but she couldn't leave until Donathan was out of the
woods.

She glanced up and noticed Sydney on full alert. Her best
friend looked desperate for answers, but she refrained from asking
her any questions. Payton rested her head in the palm of her hand,
her fingertips moving in a circular motion.

"I don't know where to begin," she said.

"At the beginning," Sydney said softly.

Payton hesitated, then took the empty seat next to her friend.

"This morning I made my way to Pittsburg because my uncle
called and was having one of his episodes. He kept talking about
someone being dead. I decided I was going to Pittsburg, and he was
going to detox once and for all. When I arrived, he was hiding along
the fence line at Jack in the Box acting unusually bizarre—"

"Why did Donathan go to Pittsburg with you?" Sydney interrupted.

"He didn't. I had no idea he would be in Pittsburg today.

After I convinced Sheldon to get in the car with me, I noticed a lot of police activity in front of the motel. Instead of merging onto the freeway, I drove by and spotted Donathan in the courtyard. He was wearing a baseball cap and sunglasses. Not really sure how he pulled that one off with all the reporters around," Payton said, her voice trailing off.

"Who was killed—and who killed them?"

"Turns out Austyn Greene is the primary suspect for the brutal murder of a tennis shoe pimp named Ray."

"Wait. Your uncle knows Austyn?"

"She's been hiding out at the motel Sheldon's been living at the past few weeks, feeding him drugs for information."

"Why?" Sydney questioned, leaning in and crossing one leg over the other.

"She believed that Sheldon knew the whereabouts of Lois Greene."

"Okay. This still doesn't explain how my husband got from the motel where the dead man was found, to having three gunshot wounds to his abdomen . . . Who shot Donathan?"

Payton could see the growing impatience in her friend, a stark contrast to the calm she exhibited just a few minutes ago.

"I'm getting to that," she said, looking away before she continued. "Curtis Holsey, the private detective Donathan hired to find Lois, knew the address of the substance abuse facility where Lois was staying. By the time we got to the location, Austyn was already in the house. I begged Donathan to wait for the police, but he decided there wasn't enough time, and he ran toward the house."

Sydney shook her head.

"A while later, police arrived on the scene, and that's when I heard multiple gunshots. SWAT stormed the house and emerged with both Donathan and Lois on stretchers."

"What about Austyn Greene? Did they catch her?"

The door to the room sprang open, and Detective McGrady, a tall lean man with perfect features, rushed in.

"There you are, Miss Jones," the detective said.

"What can I do for you *now*, Detective?" Payton said, emphasizing the word *now*. "You guys have questioned me multiple times, and I don't know anything else. Now please excuse me," Payton snapped. She was tired of the police harassing her and wanted them to leave her the hell alone.

"Did you know Raymond Carter?"

"How many times do I have to tell you, I do not know that low-life sack of shit? Now, will you please leave me alone?"

"Have you ever been inside the deceased's room at the Mar Ray Motel?" he said, closing the distance between them.

"No! I've never been inside his room."

"Ma'am, we lifted your fingerprints off some money found in the victim's room. Please stand up. I'm going to need you to come back to the police station with me to sort this out."

"What? I'm not going anywhere," Payton said, flashing back to the day she went to the motel looking for Sheldon and had given Ray a wad of cash to tell her Sheldon's whereabouts.

The detective grabbed her by the upper arm. "My request was not an option."

"You can't do this. Take your hands off of her," Sydney interjected, now standing to her feet.

Detective McGrady turned briefly and held up an authoritative hand. "Ma'am, I suggest you stay out of this unless you want to take a ride to the station, too."

He turned back to Payton, and she felt the cold stainless-steel bracelets clamp around her wrists.

"Payton Jones, you are under arrest."

EPILOGUE

Payton stared out the panoramic window mesmerized by the perimeter string lights that made Lake Merritt astonishingly beautiful at night. She raised the oversized goblet of red wine to her lips and drained the contents, showing no outward emotion from the phone call she'd just received. Donathan was finally off the ventilator, and he was going to be okay. She thought back to her arrest.

The police had practically dragged her kicking and screaming to the Pittsburg station, and she lawyered up quick, refusing to answer any more of their ridiculous questions. After all, Raymond Carter wasn't an innocent victim. He'd extorted money from her, and everybody, including the police, knew that Austyn Greene was the one responsible for that butchery. Once they checked out Tony as her alibi, she was quickly cleared as a suspect.

It still amazed her that the TSA database had been used to match her fingerprints on the money. Most people don't realize when they sign up for those frequent traveler programs that the FBI banks their fingerprints, and that database is queried as needed to solve crimes.

It had been almost a week, and still no word from Sheldon. But the three hundred bucks he took from her purse when he fled had to be gone, which meant her wayward uncle would show up soon. In all of this, the one thing she hadn't been able to shake was

staring into the eyes of her nemesis. For years, Payton had fanta-
sized about confronting Lois face-to-face. Then, on the other
hand, the thought of being in close proximity to the bitch made
her want to puke. In the moment, she blew it and was desperate
for a do-over. Her cell phone buzzed on the nightstand. She
picked it up and read the text message from Tony.

On my way up.

She smiled, then quickly replied.

Okay.

In light of what happened to his sister, Payton had seen Tony
a few times this week. During their pillow talk, she learned that
after the incident, he'd immediately placed his house on the mar-
ket, eager to sell it. He'd also flown his aunt to town to keep
Najee from being left alone. The leader of the sex trafficking ring
was dead, but the guys who had actually kidnapped his sister were
still at large. Tony believed that since they knew where they lived,
she would never be safe until they moved. Funny thing was, according to Najee, Austyn Greene was a hero. The woman had
banished her to the bathroom and demanded she stay put until the
police arrived. For that, Tony was extremely grateful.

The buzz from the doorman forced Payton away from her
thoughts. She'd tipped Samuel to let her know when Tony arrived.
Payton headed toward the living room, her bare feet sinking into
the deep pile of the carpet. She looked around the massive open
space, admiring the simple modern décor. She quickly poured herself another glass of wine and made Tony a Dangerous Consequences.

There was a light knock at the door, and she loosened the belt of
the red satin kimono robe cinched around her waist. She opened the
door, her features instantly twisting into a mix of arousal and uncer-
tainty. He was wearing all black tonight. Black jeans, black *Hamilton*
T-shirt, and a black baseball cap, and dark sunglasses hid his eyes. She
bit her bottom lip, and he smiled.

"Come in. I want to show you something."

Tony stepped inside, closed the door, and grabbed Payton by the wrist, spinning her around to face him. His hands trailed her curves covered by the satin fabric, and using her well-manicured hands, she unbuckled his belt and fondled the growing bulge in his pants. He kissed her hard and ripped the lace thong panties from her body, all the while backing her into the nearest piece of furniture. He dropped his jeans to his ankles and took a seat.

"C'mere. I want you to sit on my lap."

Seconds later, she straddled him and invited him into her heat. Payton's moans mixed with the music playing through the sound system as she rocked against him, awakening every nerve inside. He reached for her waist, and with every thrust he pulled her closer. Her groans grew louder as he matched her rhythm. He gripped her waist tighter. She moaned. He moved faster—she screamed. He nipped at her hardened nipples, and she screamed his name, coming fast and hard, the sound of both of their pleasure filling the room. Payton closed her eyes, savoring the feeling as she waited to catch her breath. Tony kissed her lips.

"Now, what do you want to show me—"

Before Payton could answer, a buzz from the doorman sounded again. Payton frowned. She'd left explicit instructions not to be disturbed once Tony arrived. Shit. Did thinking of David conjure him up unannounced? *Lord, please don't let this be David stopping by on a whim*, she prayed. Instead of answering the wall-mounted device, she picked up the handset for privacy.

"Samuel."

"Good evening, Ms. Jones. I know you said not to disturb you—"

"Yes, I do recall giving you those specific instructions," Payton said, with sarcasm oozing in her response. Tony patted her on the ass and mouthed, *"Going to the shower."*

She covered the handset speaker with her hand and said, "Coming."

"I promise you will be," Tony said before traipsing off.

"Ma'am, ma'am, are you there?

"Yes, Samuel."

"I explained to your guest that you were unavailable, but he insisted I call up, and the last thing I wanted to do was make any type of scene here in the lobby."

"Samuel, who's at the door?"

"Hold on. Let me confirm the gentleman's name—"

"Never mind," she huffed. "I'll be right down." She hung up the receiver.

She and Tony hadn't talked much about where this *thing* between them was going, but she decided to just go with it for a change, and she didn't want to screw it up.

"Shit!" Payton hissed. Who the hell did David Bryant think he was, showing up here without an invitation? She hadn't taken any of his phone calls since she'd seen him and his family at Lake Chalet, and she'd thought he would get the message.

She hurried into the bedroom and threw on some leggings, a T-shirt, and flip-flops.

"Baby, you coming?" Tony called out to her.

"Um, I have to run downstairs for a minute."

"Is everything okay? Do you need me to come with you?"

"Everything is fine. Turn on the wall jets and enjoy your shower. I'll be right back."

She grabbed her keys and wallet and took the elevator down to the lobby. The sooner she made it clear that he wasn't welcome here, the sooner she could go back upstairs to her unfinished business.

The door opened, and Payton's eyes darted left and right in search of her target, but David was nowhere to be found. She stepped up to the front desk.

"Samuel, where is my guest?"

"They stepped outside to smoke a cigarette."

" 'They'?"

"Yes, ma'am. A Mr.—"

"Sheldon Jones and Lois Greene," the familiar voice behind her said.

Payton spun around like she'd been doused with cold water. This was a fucking nightmare. Never in her wildest dreams would she have expected Sheldon to show up here. He'd only been to her condo once or twice, and that was years before. She stared at Sheldon as if he had lost his mind.

"Come over here, Niecy, and say hello to you mama."

Lois Greene stood next to him with day-old bandages and an unusual grin plastered across her face. Standing this close to her was surreal. The woman looked far worse than she did the day she'd seen her at the hospital.

"Outside. *now!*"

Payton moved quickly, and in her anger, she held the door open as the two walked out and followed her away from the building. She turned and addressed Sheldon first.

"What the hell is wrong with you? Are you high? I can't believe you've been lying to me for weeks! And you do know that I went to jail because of your bullshit. Right? And to make matters worse, you brought this conniving, thieving bitch over here, where I lay my head."

"Payton," Lois began, but her words were cut short by eyes sharp enough to cut like daggers.

"Don't you dare say my name, you ruthless, good-for-nothing, thieving whore!" she spat. "You don't have the right to refer to yourself as my mother ever again. You lost that privilege when you left me standing in front of that movie theater twenty-five years ago. Now, I need both of you to take your sorry asses back to wherever the hell you came from and don't ever darken my door again—"

"I ain't going nowhere until you give me my goddamn money," Sheldon interrupted, slurring his words, making his mouth sound like it was full of marbles.

Payton opened her wallet to retrieve the cash she had on hand. If a few dollars could make this little duo go poof until she could figure out what to do next, then so be it. She glanced at Lois, subliminally daring her to move, then tossed all the bills she had in

Sheldon's direction. They both looked down on him as he scrambled to pick the money up.

"This is all the cash I have," Payton said. "I'll give you a call first thing tomorrow to get you the rest. After that, I want you to take your money and stay the fuck out of my life."

Keep reading to see where it all began
With an excerpt from
DANGEROUS CONSEQUENCES
Available now
Wherever books are sold

CHAPTER 1

Dr. Sydney Marie James panicked as her BlackBerry slipped out of her grasp and landed on the floor close to the front passenger door.

"Shit!" she yelled. She could hear the exchange operator's distant voice saying, "Hello? Hello?" But short of unlocking her seat belt and climbing across the seat to retrieve the phone, there was nothing she could do. She was en route to Children's Hospital, initially on her way to work, but now she was responding to the trauma call she'd just received for an infant who needed immediate neurosurgery. Frustrated, she yelled into the confines of her SUV.

"Hello. This is Dr. James. I've dropped my BlackBerry and can't pick it up because I'm driving. But I'm on my way and should arrive at the hospital in about fifteen minutes." She had no idea whether the operator could hear her, but it was worth a try.

The traffic ahead crawled along. Morning commuters on their way to work congested the I-580 inlet that would take her toward downtown Oakland, making traffic a nightmare.

"Come on," Sydney hissed and blew her horn in irritation. Fresh perspiration trickled down her spine and mingled with the aging perspiration from her morning run. She was still dressed in black running tights, Saucony running shoes, and her favorite UCLA sweatshirt. She'd run her usual six-mile route at the Berkeley Marina, with the morning mist plummeting down onto her skin and a cluster of squawking seagulls out scavenging for any sign of food lulling her with their singsong pitch, which had helped to clear her mind. But that was forty minutes ago, when her world seemed peaceful and serene . . . before she received the emergency call during rush-hour traffic.

She took her eyes off the road for a brief second to search the passenger seat littered with CDs. She wanted to hear a Ledisi song, the one she'd played while making love to Donathan earlier and during their romantic getaway at the Highlands Inn in Carmel. The soulful music soothed her, which was what she needed on most days while commuting from El Cerrito to Oakland in the bumper-to-bumper traffic.

A gap in the blockage opened up. Sydney pushed hard on the accelerator, hoping that she wouldn't run into another obstruction farther ahead. She had no idea which of her colleagues was on duty. It was probably Julia Stevens. But if Julia started surgery on the incoming patient, she would be required to complete it, adding additional hours to her already-long shift. Frantic to reach the hospital, Sydney drove in an unforgiving manner as drivers on either side of her attempted to jump out of their slow-moving lanes and into hers.

"Not today, people!" Sydney bellowed. She accelerated in an attempt to prevent a red Nissan pickup truck carrying lawn-care equipment from swerving in front of her.

The traffic came to a sudden halt. Realizing she was about to crash into a sea of stationary cars, Sydney instinctively slammed on the brake pedal with both feet and held her breath as she heard the tires screeching and smelled burning rubber. Her Range Rover came to a complete stop without a collision.

"Thank God," she exhaled, releasing her tight grip on the steering wheel.

Then the scream of another set of tires, a loud thud, and the sound of shattering glass punched Sydney in the center of her back. Dazed, she moved her damp, dark brown hair out of her eyes and noticed light blue smoke merging with the morning smog, along with the overpowering odor of overheating antifreeze billowing past her windows. She peered into her rearview mirror and saw a Hispanic man getting out of the red Nissan pickup she'd earlier prevented from cutting in front of her. She watched the man walk to the rear of his truck, reach into the truck bed, and remove a shovel, knocking it against the lawn mowers, the noise loud enough to make her jump. Then he hastily approached her, swinging the shovel at the air.

"Estupid pendeja! I can't believe you just made me wreck my work truck," yelled the man in a Spanish accent as thick as the fog that blanketed the San Francisco Bay.

"Get out of the car, you *pinche puta!"* He slapped Sydney's car window with the open palm of his thick, callused hand. The contact echoed loudly inside the car.

Intimidated by the force and vulgarity of the man's anger, Sydney stared at him through the speckles of spit on the glass that separated them. Bulging muscle cords in his neck and trickles of blood running down his forehead and pooling at his neatly trimmed mustache pointed downward to the shovel dangling from his left hand.

As bile rose in Sydney's throat, she attempted to calm down and think rationally. She glanced at the passing commuters, praying for someone to stop and help her. Instead, she found a string of spectators hoping the drama would unfold before they crept completely by and missed it.

"Open the fucking door!" the man blurted as he yanked on the door handle.

Her eyes glanced at the clock, then to the phone. She needed to call for help.

"Get the fuck away from my car," Sydney barked, hoping her angry words would bring this man to his senses.

"I'm not playing around, lady." The man began jerking on the door so hard that her car rocked. She unfastened her seat belt, climbed across the middle console, and retrieved the phone from the floor. She was so nervous that, instead of dialing 911, she dialed her husband. He answered after the first ring.

"I must have dicked you down well this—"

"Donathan!" Sydney screamed into the phone.

"Get out of the car, you *pinche puta!*" The Hispanic man continued his tirade, drifting in and out of his native tongue. Holding the shovel high above his head with both hands, he slammed it into the hood, repeating his assault over and over again.

"Get away from my damn car." The loud thud of the shovel hitting the hood registered through the phone.

"Sydney, who is that? Where are you?" Donathan demanded.

"I was just rear-ended by this man, and he's—"

"I'm going to fuck you up just like you fucked up my truck. Get out, *pendeja*, before I smash your windows." Sydney scrambled for her purse on the back seat. She reached inside and pulled out an old canister of pepper spray that she'd hoped she'd never have to use.

"Where are you?" Donathan demanded again.

"I-I'm on I-80, about to merge onto 580." The hood of the truck absorbed another hit from the shovel.

Her eyes went wide as the man shouldered the shovel and paralleled his feet, like he was Barry Bonds readying his swing and his strike zone was now the front windshield of the Range Rover.

"Oh, God, noooooooooooooooooo!"

CHAPTER 2

Frazzled, Sydney stood on the shoulder of the road as she spoke into her cell phone to the exchange operator. "I'll live."

Five vehicles were parked next to the guardrail, including two highway patrol cruisers. Sydney's eyes were fixed on the Hispanic man being stuffed into the back seat of the police car. He was clad in jeans, cowboy boots, and a plaid button-down shirt, his hair short, neatly trimmed above his ears. He looked like a normal guy, but where normal people radiated a sense of calm, this man was pulsating with anger.

When Donathan maneuvered his Harley onto the shoulder, Sydney ended her call with the hospital and watched as he parked and removed his helmet. His face was tense, and his forehead furrowed as he got off the motorcycle and made his way over to her.

"Are you okay?" Donathan asked, his eyes narrowed in confusion. He stole a glimpse of the hood, then pulled her into his embrace.

"Punk motherfucker," he mumbled under his breath. His tone was seething and harsh. She could feel his heart beating like it wanted to jump out of his chest, which matched the beat of her own. The possibility of becoming a road-rage statistic disturbed her as she listened to the two African American males in their mid-twenties give their statements to the officers. They'd arrived just in time to subdue the Hispanic man before he broke out the windshield with the shovel.

"What happened?" Donathan questioned, his voice quivering with the fury he wanted to unleash.

"Honey, I'm fine. I just happened to be on the highway in front of a lunatic this morning."

Sydney rubbed her hand across her upper chest region, where the seat belt had pressed into her during impact. As she took a peek inside her sweatshirt, Donathan's eyes followed. The couple stared at an almost two-inch-wide bruise that reminded her of a beauty pageant sash. "You need to get that checked out—"

"It's just a bruise from the seat belt," she said. "No big deal. I'm fine."

"Sydney, don't give me that 'I'm fine' crap. You might have fractured your collarbone."

In defense, she raised both hands. "Calm down, sweetie. I'll let one of my colleagues check me out when I get to the hospital."

"Excuse me, Dr. James," one of the officers said, interrupting their battle of wills. "Here's my card. I've written the incident report number on the back. It will be a few days before the report is ready, but if you provide this number to your insurance agency, they will be able to obtain all the information they need. The district attorney will contact you soon to discuss the possibility of filing charges. All I need is your signature on this preliminary report and you are free to go."

"File charges?"

"Yes, ma'am. In cases like this, that's procedure."

"Well, what if I don't want to file charges?"

"Of course, she wants to file charges," Donathan interrupted, his face twisted with confusion. He stretched his hand toward the highway patrolman. "Thanks, Officer."

"No problem, sir, glad we were all able to walk away without any casualties. Now, if you can just sign right here, Dr. James, you can be on your way." Sydney nodded with understanding, took the clipboard from the officer, and scribbled her name.

Donathan made his way over to the two Good Samaritans and thanked them. Sydney stood still for a moment. *Was her erratic and aggressive driving the cause of the accident?* As she headed toward her SUV, a wave of panic washed over her, and her hands shook as she buckled herself in. What would have happened to her had the Hispanic man actually gotten her out of the vehicle? Would he have hit her with the shovel? She could be dead. Her momentary theory of being responsible for the accident dissolved. She might have driven a bit erratically to prevent the man from cutting in front of her, but by no means was she the reason he rear-ended her.

Donathan approached the driver's side window. "Are you sure it's drivable? We should have the highway patrol officer call a tow truck—"

"Babe, I really don't have time for that. I need to get to the hospital. The dents on the hood are from his shovel, not the impact, so it should drive okay." One turn of the key and the engine hummed to life. "See, it sounds great."

After a moment of hesitation, Donathan conceded, and then leaned over the window to kiss her. "I'll see you this evening."

Sydney took a deep breath and watched in the rearview mirror as her husband walked away.

After a few false starts, Sydney pulled away from the shoulder into the oncoming traffic. She carefully negotiated the lane switches until she was in the farthest left lane, then refocused her attention on getting to the hospital. She turned up the volume on the sound system and sang out loud, trying to forget the horror of what had just happened to her.

The bright red Emergency Medical Service helicopter was lifting off the landing pad by the time Sydney entered the doctors' parking lot at Children's Hospital. She killed the ignition and cut short her duet with Mary J. Blige. After she retrieved her gym bag from the back seat, Albert, the security guard, appeared out of nowhere.

"Morning, Dr. James."

Sydney grabbed her chest. "Albert, you scared the shit out of me," she said before she climbed out of the driver's seat and closed the door behind her.

"Sorry about that, Dr. James. Dr. Stevens mentioned you'd had an accident." He stepped forward to examine the damage to the hood of the vehicle. Sydney had worked at the hospital for three years and was very familiar with the security staff. When she worked overnight shifts, Albert always made sure she got to her car safely.

Sydney glanced at the speckles of dried spit on the driver's side window.

"Other than my bruised ego and being late for work, I'm fine, Albert," she answered, and rushed through the secured entrance, checking her watch as the elevator doors closed behind her. It had been almost three hours since her shift began. She exited the elevator on the fifth floor and never looked up. Her subconscious mind guided the way to the doctors' lounge.

Minutes later, freshly showered and ready to begin her rounds, Sydney strolled down the corridor outlined by the dark blue baseboards and nursery rhyme murals of stars, cows, and moons. She stopped at the nurses' station, but before she retrieved her clipboard, she stretched her arms above her head, twisting from side to side to relieve the tension in her middle back. Her private cell phone vibrated inside her pocket. She looked at the screen, but she didn't recognize the number. "Sydney James," she answered.

"Sydney, is that you, babe?" the familiar yet unidentifiable voice said anxiously. "This is your neighbor, Barbara Brown, from across the street and—"

"Mrs. Brown, is everything okay?"

A clear image of her meddlesome neighbor took shape in her mind. Sydney was raised to respect her elders, but Mrs. Brown constantly tried her patience. If you looked up "nosy" in the dictionary, Mrs. Brown's picture would be right there.

"Hon, your house alarm went off about an hour ago, so I called the police. They're here now to check it out."

Sydney glanced at her watch.

"I told the police that you and Donathan were out of town and wouldn't be returning for a few more days, so I—"

"Mrs. Brown, we came back from Carmel last night. Donathan should be at home now."

"Well, I told Herbert that's what I thought." Her voice trailed off as she processed what she'd just said. "But I haven't seen Donathan since you left."

Sydney shook her head in disbelief. She wasn't in the mood for a dose of Mrs. Brown and her antics today.

"Well, you gave me this number and told me to call you if there was ever a problem, and since I ain't seen a hair of your husband since you left—"

"Mrs. Brown, is the alarm still going off? What is it that the officers need?" Sydney struggled to keep the impatience out of her voice.

"Well, they just need to verify things are okay. I didn't want anything to happen to your house while you were away, so when I heard that alarm go off, I told Herbert I was going to call the police. I didn't want you to come home and all your belongings be gone."

Sydney rolled her eyes upward and sighed. Gone? There was no way anyone was going to get anything out of the house without Mrs. Brown seeing or hearing something. She pulled at the black elastic band that held her hair in a ponytail. It was giving her a headache.

"Mrs. Brown, thank you for looking out for us. We really appreciate it."

"Is there a number for Donathan that you want me to give to them?"

"No, ma'am, I'm going to hang up and give him a call now."

"Alright then, sugah, you do that."

Sydney ended the call and immediately dialed her home number. Donathan picked up on the first ring.

"Hey, boo," she whispered into the phone as she headed down the hallway toward the neonatal intensive care unit. "I just got off the phone with Mrs. Brown. Apparently, the alarm went off about an hour ago and she called the police. They're outside responding to her call."

"I set it off when I left earlier, but the alarm company called, and I took care of it. I swear, that lady has got too much time on her hands."

"I know, but at least she's watching the house."

"More like watching other folks' business." He chuckled. "I don't understand why she called the police because if she heard the alarm going off, she definitely had to hear me leave on the motorcycle. Did you get checked out yet?"

"I'm starting my rounds now, but I promise to let someone look at me soon."

"You know, you could come back home, and I'd be happy to check you out thoroughly myself."

"Don't tempt me."

"Well, I guess I'll have to wait until tonight to do my inspection."

Sydney giggled.

"Alright, babe. I'm on my way out to talk to the men in blue."

"Okay."

After saying goodbye a second time, Sydney hurried down the hall and bumped into Dr. Miles Day exiting the double doors that led to the NICU. Miles was new to the neurosurgery team at Children's, having only worked at the hospital for two months. In that short period of time, he had the female nurses taking bets on which one was going to run their fingers through the perfect-sized dreadlocks that rested neatly at the nape of his neck and which one was going to get in his bed first.

"You're definitely a sight for tired eyes," he said warmly. She flashed him a brilliant smile in return.

His six-foot-four lean, muscular frame towered over her. He was already dressed in street clothes underneath his lab coat—a black Ralph Lauren T-shirt, with the signature red polo horse, and expensive black slacks tailored to fall just above his Gucci sneakers. He fastened his eyes on the V-neck of her scrubs, skimmed her entire body, then took a slow return trip back to her face. Instinctively, Sydney drew her hand to the bruise across her chest.

"I appreciate you covering for me."

"If the tables were turned, I'm sure you would have done the same." His eyes focused on the bruise. "Are you okay?"

"My collarbone is a little tender. When I get a chance, I'll run down to the imaging department and have someone take an X-ray."

"Would you like me to do that for you?"

"No. I've kept you here long enough. I'll wait until things settle down a bit, then I'll get someone to take care of it. So, what did I miss?"

"A baby girl, last name Perkins, born with spina bifida. Birth by C-section, near full-term, but she weighed about four pounds, one ounce. She was transported here by helicopter from John Muir Medical Center in Walnut Creek. The opening level was an approximate L1, and the long-term prognosis does not look good," Miles recited.

"Have you spoken with the parents yet?"

"The mother is still hospitalized at John Muir. There was no mention of a father. The baby arrived alone."

Sydney felt a sudden sadness. As a pediatric neurosurgeon, having to be the one who shattered parents' dreams for their children was the most difficult part of her job. She couldn't imagine being a mother, especially a single mother, learning that her child would face lifelong medical challenges and being helpless to do anything about it. She forced a smile and changed the subject. "How about I buy you an early lunch?"

A coy smile played at the corners of his mouth.

"Food sounds wonderful right about now, but I have to take a rain check. I was just about to cancel my Comcast installation for this afternoon, but since you're here, I think I can still make it to my loft in time for the appointment. I've watched the *Love Jones* and *Boomerang* DVDs so much in the last two months that I know every single word, and that's scary." They laughed in unison.

"A rain check it is, then. Maybe we can go someplace other than the hospital cafeteria and I can bring along my girlfriend, Payton."

Sydney watched Miles closely as he smothered a groan and shook his head. He'd transferred here from Chicago a couple of months ago, and she guessed his reaction was related to the residual effects of other staff members trying to make a love connection for him. Miles certainly didn't look like he needed any help in that department.

"I think you would like her."

Miles lowered his head, and a hint of a smile exposed his dimples.

"She's a very attractive woman," Sydney said convincingly.

He held the door to the NICU open, making room for Sydney to pass under his makeshift bridge. Their pagers went off in unison. He spoke first.

"It's probably the Perkins baby. C'mon, I'll help you get started."

Sydney shook her head. "Miles, you go home. You've already been here for sixteen hours and you look exhausted. If I need an extra hand, Julia can help me."

Miles clipped his pager back onto his belt. "I really don't mind."

"Didn't you just say you had a Comcast appointment to keep?"

Miles nodded and smiled. "Yeah, I do. But call me if you need me," he said, before he turned on his heels and disappeared down the corridor.

As the double doors of the NICU closed behind her, Sydney found herself bombarded with the synchronized sounds of mechanical breathing. The space was large, with a circular nurses' station situated in the middle of the room. Multicolored lifelines attached to the tiny incubators were visible, and regulated beeps filled the room. Her eyes locked on a young couple standing over a tiny infant lying on her back. The child was motionless—a girl, she guessed by the pink cap that rested beside her in the clear bassinette. Her head was wrapped snugly with gauze to stabilize the IV inserted in the vein that ran down the front of her forehead. The mother was on one side, gently brushing her finger along the side of the baby's cheek, and the father on the other side rested his index finger in the baby's tiny palm. Sydney felt sad. Most of the babies in NICU had somebody who cared about them, but there were others who had not been touched or held by anyone other than doctors and nurses in weeks.

"Over here, Dr. James," one of the nurses called, seizing her attention.

Sydney made her way across the aisle, gazed down at the baby, and sighed before removing the stethoscope from her coat pocket. She hoped there was something she could do to make life more bearable for the baby, even if it was only for a little while.

Connect with 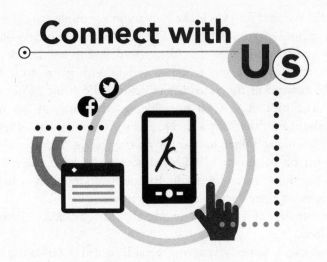 Us

Visit us online at
KensingtonBooks.com
to read more from your favorite authors, see books
by series, view reading group guides, and more.

Join us on social media

for sneak peeks, chances to win books and prize packs,
and to share your thoughts with other readers.

facebook.com/kensingtonpublishing
twitter.com/kensingtonbooks

Tell us what you think!

To share your thoughts, submit a review,
or sign up for our eNewsletters, please visit:
KensingtonBooks.com/TellUs.